It was almost *challenging* to think that what he had missed first time round could now be his.

Dark, speculative eyes drifted down to the shape of Lucy's small, high breasts, and Gabriel's arousal was as fierce as it was sudden.

Lucy was disconcerted by that lazy appraisal in Gabriel's roving dark eyes. It made her feel uncomfortable. She suppressed the crazy notion that buried beneath that discomfort a slow swirl of excitement was eddying in her veins, making her breasts tingle and sending a shooting, melting warmth between her legs.

'And what do you have in mind?'

'You. I have *you* in mind.'

Cathy Williams is originally from Trinidad, but has lived in England for a number of years. She currently has a house in Warwickshire, which she shares with her husband Richard, her three daughters, Charlotte, Olivia and Emma, and their pet cat, Salem. She adores writing romantic fiction, and would love one of her girls to become a writer—although at the moment she is happy enough if they do their homework and agree not to bicker with one another!

Recent titles by the same author:

A TEMPESTUOUS TEMPTATION
THE GIRL HE'D OVERLOOKED
THE TRUTH BEHIND HIS TOUCH
THE SECRET SINCLAIR

THE NOTORIOUS GABRIEL DIAZ

BY

CATHY WILLIAMS

First published in Great Britain 2013
by Mills & Boon, an imprint of Harlequin (UK) Limited.
Harlequin (UK) Limited, Eton House, 18-24 Paradise Road,
Richmond, Surrey TW9 1SR

ISBN: 978 0 263 89988 7

Harlequin (UK) policy is to use papers that are natural, renewable and recyclable products and made from wood grown in sustainable forests. The logging and manufacturing process conform to the legal environmental regulations of the country of origin.

Printed and bound in Spain
by Blackprint CPI, Barcelona

THE NOTORIOUS GABRIEL DIAZ

CHAPTER ONE

'WHAT DO YOU *mean*? Explain again. I'm not getting it.' Lucy Robins looked between her parents, buying time while her brain tried to catch up with what she had just been told. Running round and round at her feet, Freddy, the pug she had adopted three years ago, now made a stab at grabbing her attention by flipping over on his back and playing dead.

'Not now, Freddy!' she said, patting her lap. With that small show of encouragement, the brown and black dog scrambled onto her lap and proceeded to gaze adoringly up at her.

The second Lucy had got her mother's phone call she had known something was wrong. Celia Robins never called her daughter at work, even though Lucy had repeatedly told her that it really didn't matter—that it wasn't as though she worked in an office where there was a big, bad boss keeping a watchful eye over employees and punishing anyone caught using their mobile.

The huge garden centre, set within the grounds of botanical gardens, which drew visitors from the across the country, was the most relaxed of environments. There, Lucy was part-gardener, helping with the landscaping team, and part-artist, using her newly gained degree in graphic art to draw exquisite detailed illustrations of flowers for a comprehensive book of the flora and fauna at the centre.

Her mother's call had come just as she had been about to start replanting a batch of delicate orchids that had been meticulously cared for since their arrival at the centre six months previously. She had heard the words, *'Honey, could you possibly come home? There's something of an emergency...'* and had flown to her car, pausing only to tell Victor where she was going and to scoop up Freddy, who was allowed free rein in the outdoor space.

Now she stared in dismay at her father's drooping figure. 'What do you mean you're in trouble with the company finances?'

Nicholas Robins, as small and round as his wife was tall and slender, raised apologetic eyes to his daughter. 'I borrowed some money a few years ago, Luce. Not much. When your mother had her stroke…things just got a little crazy… I thought we were going to lose her… I wanted to give her her dream of a cruise… I wasn't thinking rationally…'

On her lap, Freddy had nodded off and was snoring. Lucy stroked his fat tummy. Her skin was clammy. When her father had announced that he and her mother were going on a cruise—a lifetime dream, a wonderful opportunity that might be their last—he had told her he had received an unexpected bonus at work. The company had just been taken over by an electronics giant and Lucy had believed him—had been over the moon at his unexpected good luck.

'When she recovered—' her father's voice was laboured, heavy '—I wanted to take her somewhere special. I thought if I borrowed a little bit more I could repay it before it was missed. I can't believe I was that stupid.'

Lucy glanced worriedly towards her mother. Celia Robins was a frail woman who would be unable to cope with the distressing catastrophe unfolding in front of her. The stroke she had suffered had sapped her of her energy, and both Lucy and her father lived in constant fear that she would suffer another.

'I didn't think that anything would change after GGD took us over,' her father continued in a shaking voice. 'Before the takeover, I was the only bookkeeper there. They brought in a team of financial whiz kids. I managed to keep things under wraps for as long as I could, and I'd started repaying the money, but this morning I was called in and told they had found some discrepancies and that it might be an idea if I took a little leave until it gets sorted out….'

Appalled, Lucy didn't know what to say. Her father was by no means a crook, and yet she knew with a sinking heart that no lawyer in the land would see it that way. He had helped himself to company funds and that was where the story would end. There would be no room for sob stories or excuses. That wasn't how big organisations operated. Especially that would not be how GGD would operate.

Gabriel Garcia Diaz was the guy who had founded GGD. Ruthless, cold and brilliant, he had risen to dominate the field of electronics in the space of a mere eight years, consuming smaller companies and growing more and more powerful in the process. Gabriel Garcia Diaz was the shark in the pond, and a shark wouldn't look at small minnows like her father and weep tears of sympathy for his plight.

A wash of nervous perspiration broke out over her. For the past two years she had contrived to put Gabriel Diaz out of her mind, but now the past galloped towards her, stampeding into the present and crashing through the flimsy defences she had erected to keep the unsettling memory of him at bay.

She had met him quite by accident. For weeks the talk of the town had been the takeover of Sims Electronics by GGD. The big guns were rolling into town and would be rescuing the ailing company where her father worked, transforming it into a mega-sized giant and in the process creating hundreds of jobs.

Lucy hadn't been able to get worked up over it. She'd been pleased that the rampant unemployment that afflicted their little slice of Somerset would be brought to an end, but big business didn't interest her. She had just got her job at the garden centre and all her excitement had been saved for that. She loved plants, she loved working outdoors, and she'd also had something else to celebrate. She had been called in and offered the task of illustrating the centre's first documented book of all the rare and exotic species of flowers being cultivated in the massive greenhouses.

Indeed, she had forgotten that the big boss of GGD would be rolling into town. Excited to tell her father about her new area of responsibility, for both her parents knew how keen she was to utilise her art degree, she had hopped on her bike in her lunch hour and cycled like the wind to where he worked.

It had only been when she had spotted the sleek black limo and the convoy of similarly grand cars in the parking lot that she'd belatedly remembered that it was the big day.

In the glittering summer sun, all the employees of Sims had gathered outside the building while, dominating the space in the centre, and surrounded by an alarming circle of threatening men in dark suits, one man had stood literally head and shoulders above the rest.

Lucy's eyes had been drawn to him, and even from a safe distance she'd been able to feel the power of his personality radiating out with shocking force. Everyone's attention had been glued to his face. Some of them had had their mouths half open, in thrall to whatever he was saying. She hadn't been able to hear. She'd been too far away. However, she'd understood what it was about the man that commanded their attention. Beyond the aura of power he was just the most incredible human being she had ever clapped eyes on. Tall, with raven-black hair, harsh, beautifully chiselled features and a bronzed colouring that lent him the air of someone breathtakingly exotic, he was as spectacularly beautiful as a lovingly carved statue of a Greek god.

Her father had been in the inner circle, dressed in his best suit, but as the tall man had headed to the open doors of the company, surrounded by his entourage, her father had fallen back and she'd taken the chance to race towards him on her bike so that she could tell him her good news.

Mr VIP had been heading off to inspect the building and the components centre. Later, Lucy hadn't understood how it was that he had managed to notice her amidst the excited commotion surrounding him. Had he spotted her cycling away? Had he radioed one of his lackeys who had remained outside with the fleet of cars, primed for a hasty departure? Nor, at the time, had she thought anything of the beefy guy in the suit who'd asked her who she was and what she was doing on the premises.

Anxious not to mention any connection with her father, for she didn't know if it was against rules for employees to speak when their attention should be one hundred percent focused on their leader, Lucy had instead vaguely told him that she worked at the garden centre and had been checking to make sure all the plants they'd installed for the visit were okay.

Later, packing up for the day, she had had her first real contact with Gabriel Garcia Diaz. About to cycle home, she had been bending down to the wheel lock on the bike.

When she'd stood up, there he'd been. At a distance, two bodyguards had lounged by a shiny black car.

He had literally taken her breath away. Never had she felt such a strange compulsion to stare and stare and stare—as though her eyes couldn't get their fill of his bronzed, exotic beauty. Up close he'd been so much more breathtaking, and when he'd spoken, his voice had been a low, dark, lazy drawl…asking her to tell him her name… telling her that he had noticed her…informing her that he hadn't planned on staying over but he would now make an exception to take her out….

Lucy had been speechless, flustered and vaguely terrified. What sort of man approached a woman he didn't know and informed her that she would be taken out to dinner? In a tone of voice that denied any negative response?

His urbane sophistication, his staggering good looks, and the lazy, sexual appreciation in those dark, dark eyes had made her head swim. Backing away, she had turned him down. She hadn't been able to imagine what a man like him would want with someone like her, but as soon as she'd asked herself the question she'd come up with the answer. *Sex*.

She had virtually run for cover and had continued to turn him down for the remainder of that week, which had seen deliveries of flowers—terrifically expensive flowers, the centre of attention at the garden centre—and one express delivery of a gold bracelet that she had refused to accept. He hadn't approached her again in person, but the sustained bombardment, designed to erode her defences, had confused her and sent her further into hiding. In the end she had left a text message on the cell number he had given her. She had told him to go away, that she had a boyfriend…

And he had.

Curiously, the abrupt cessation of all that attention had left her feeling deflated for weeks afterwards. Then, gradually, she had gathered herself and put the memory of him behind her as just one of those weird things.

Working at the garden centre left her no time to question the disturbing impact he had had on her. Nor had he returned to visit the offices where her father continued to work. Huge though the modernisations and expansions had been to Sims, it remained, or so she had been told, just a very small tentacle of one mammoth conglomerate.

Now, as Lucy looked at her parents, who seemed frightened and diminished by the rapidity with which everything they knew seemed to be unravelling, the image of Gabriel Diaz rose up in her head like a dark, avenging angel.

'Perhaps I could help,' she offered, her heart beating nervously. 'I mean, I get a good salary at the garden centre, and I could always ask whether they would advance me some of the money for the illustrations I've already done for their second volume. I'm nearly through with them. I'm sure they wouldn't mind.... Plus Kew Gardens are interested in commissioning me to do some work for them....'

'It's no good, honey.' Nicholas Robins shook his head with something approaching despair. 'I tried to talk to them...to explain the circumstances. I offered to have my salary cut by as much as it took to pay the debt off but they weren't interested. They said that's not how they run their organisation. One strike and you're out.'

'And you spoke to...to...Mr Diaz himself?' His name passing her lips sent a shiver through her, and again she recalled those glittering, mesmerising dark eyes and the way they had looked at her.

'Oh, no.' Her father sighed. 'I asked if I could see him but this matter isn't important enough for *him* to get involved. The man's hardly in the country as it is.'

'So what's going to happen?' Lucy could barely phrase the question because she was so scared of the answer, but ducking reality was never a good idea. Her voice was thick with tears but she wouldn't let herself cry. Her parents were both distressed enough as it was. She was an only child, and they had had her late in life and always protected her. Her unhappiness would be as wounding to them as their own.

'At best,' her father confessed, 'we'll lose the roof over our heads. At worst…'

That dreadful worst-case scenario remained unspoken, but it hovered in the air like a malignant cloud. At worst he could go to jail. Embezzlement was an offence that the courts took very seriously.

Lucy opened her mouth to suggest that they could both always come and live with her, sell their house and beg to pay off the debt with the proceeds, but practically how on earth would that work? She rented a small one-bedroomed cottage on the edge of the village. It suited her needs ideally, with its big, rambling garden and a tiny studio off the kitchen, where she often worked at her illustrations at night, but at best it was only good to house one girl and her dog. Stick two more human beings in and there wouldn't be room to move.

The options were running out fast. Her mother rose to make them all another pot of tea, and in her absence Lucy leaned forward and hurriedly asked how her mother was doing. *Really.*

'I'm worried,' her father said unhappily. 'She's being supportive but she has to be scared stiff. And we both know her health isn't good. If I get put away you'll have to look after her, Luce. She can't look after herself….'

'You won't get put away!' But the sound of options running out was the sound of jail doors being clanged shut. 'I could have a word….' she said finally.

'With who, my darling? Believe me, I've tried my damnedest and they're not interested. I even offered to show them receipts for how the money was spent…the holiday Mum and I took after she had the stroke…. They don't care. They're there to do a job and there's no appealing to them….'

'I could see Mr Diaz…'

'My love, he'll be a hundred times worse. He's a money-making machine without an emotional bone in his body. Sims went from being a small, friendly family firm to being part of a giant company where profits get made but there's a price to be paid. There's no such thing as compassionate leave. He has his minions there to make sure no one leaves early or even makes personal calls….'

Lucy thought back to that broodingly arrogant face and could well believe that anyone daring to disobey Gabriel Diaz would be hung, drawn and quartered without trial.

And yet he had sought her out two years ago, had made his intentions perfectly clear. He had wanted her. She hadn't understood why at the time, and she was no nearer to understanding now, but couldn't that brief flare of attraction help her out now? Perhaps encourage him to be more sympathetic to her parents' plight than he might normally have been under the circumstances?

Glancing up, Lucy caught sight of herself in the long oval mirror over the fireplace. What she saw was a slender girl with waist-length fair hair the colour of vanilla ice cream streaked with toffee, at the moment swept back into a haphazard ponytail, a heart-shaped face and green eyes. There was nothing there to get excited about as far as she was concerned, and chances were that the man wouldn't even remember who she was, but wasn't it worth the risk of approaching him?

'Let me think about things, Dad,' she told him, moving to where he was slumped on the sofa to give him a hug. 'I'll see what I can do. I'll try and get to Mr Diaz… you can never tell…'

She was thankful that her parents knew nothing of that peculiar little episode two years ago. Had they known that the devil in disguise had made a pass at her they would have immediately forbidden any contact. They were deeply traditional and would have been appalled to think that she might be allowed entry to Gabriel Diaz's hallowed walls simply because he had once fancied her for a week.

As it was, they did their best over the next hour to drop the conversation, to talk about less contentious topics, but by the time Lucy left later that evening she was drained, and so scared on behalf of her parents that she almost couldn't think clearly.

Not even the soothing act of drawing could calm her tumultuous thoughts and Freddy, sensing her mood, trotted behind her with a forlorn look on his squashy little face, the very picture of a depressed mutt.

The following morning she didn't give herself a chance to argue her way out of what she knew she had to do. Instead she phoned the garden centre first thing and explained that she wouldn't be coming in. She didn't anticipate being in London longer than a couple of hours, but Freddy would have to be deprived of his day dashing around the gardens, chasing insects. He gazed at her reproachfully as she closed the front door on him, immune to her promises of a treat when she returned.

It was warm outside. Summer had arrived with a bounce, delivering blue, cloudless skies for the past three weeks, and today was no exception.

It was a shame that she had no attractive dresses to wear to a meeting she suspected would be grueling—if it even took place at all. As her father had said, Gabriel Diaz was out of the country most of the time. Working at the garden centre had made her lazy when it came to her wardrobe. There was no need for her to wear anything dressy, so she had a cupboard that was full to bursting with faded jeans, combat trousers, jumpers, T-shirts and overalls.

She chose the least worn of her jeans, one of the few T-shirts that didn't advertise a rock band, and the most respectable of her shoes—a pair of black flats.

The mirror reflected back to her a picture of a girl, five foot eight, slender to the point of skinny, with long blond hair, which she personally considered her best feature. As a last resort, to add glamour to the package, but feeling tainted by the very act of aiming to appeal to someone via her looks, she dabbed on a little lip gloss. That, however, was as far as she was prepared to go.

In the middle of concluding a distasteful conversation with a certain tall, sexy brunette model he had been seeing for the past four months, and whose presence in his life had now outstayed its welcome, Gabriel Diaz was interrupted by his secretary poking her head into his office to tell him that he had a visitor.

'Name?'

'She refused to say,' Nicolette said apologetically. 'She said it's personal. I could tell her that you're not in...'

In receipt of information like that, Gabriel's first response would usually have been to assume that the woman in question was a lover. Despite his dislike of any woman intruding in his workspace, it had been known to happen. Women had an irritating tendency to think that sex bought them leniency in certain areas—to imagine that sleeping with him entitled them to pop into his office for nothing more than a quick chat. Gabriel could have told them that such behaviour only guaranteed an early exit from his life.

But having just come off the phone with Imogen, he knew that his mood was not conducive to completing the report that was blinking at him on his computer.

He berated himself for not taking action sooner to terminate his relationship with Imogen. Glamorous she might very well be, but she had displayed sufficient signs of clinginess early on for him to have realised that whatever they had would end in tears. Sure enough, the fifteen-minute telephone conversation he had just had with her had been ample proof that her expectations had far exceeded what had been on offer.

This was the third woman Gabriel had had in eight months. Even for him that was a record. What was it about women who just never seemed to get the message that he wasn't in it for the long haul? It wasn't as though he didn't make it clear to them from the very beginning that he was not a man who was on the lookout for commitment. No one could ever accuse him of not being scrupulously fair on that front. He never, *ever* made promises he had no intention of keeping. And yet time and again what started out as something light-hearted and fun ended up with him having to wriggle away from a woman who'd begun taking an unhealthy interest in domestic life and an even more unhealthy interest in diamond rings and friends with babies.

He scowled at the memory of Imogen shrieking down the phone that he had led her on. Such behaviour disgusted Gabriel. And he found it particularly annoying that she had seen fit to call him at work.

Faced with the prospect of being distracted from his report or seeing a mystery woman for ten minutes, he decided that bit of light relief might do the trick.

'Show her up.' He sat back and braced himself for someone on a begging mission. 'But make sure you tell her that I have ten minutes to spare and no more. Oh, and Nicolette? Remind her that I already contribute heavily to a number of charities. The money pit isn't bottomless….'

Hovering on the ground floor, where all the marble and glass and chrome and well-groomed artificial plants were combining to send her blood pressure shooting through the roof, Lucy was trying hard not to panic.

A surprise visit to Gabriel Diaz had seemed such a good idea at the time. In fact, it had seemed like the *only* idea at the time. But now a serious case of nerves was threatening to make her turn tail and flee.

The building, which she had located in the labyrinth of office buildings in the heart of the City, was terrifyingly impressive. Everyone at Sims had been thrilled to death when their small two-storeyed brick-clad office block had been expanded and turned into a high-tech glasshouse. Her father had related numerous tales of clean tiled floors and brand-new top-of-the-range desks. Lucy thought that he would be rendered speechless were he to see the opulence of DGG headquarters.

She had almost expected to be told that Gabriel wasn't in the country, and she told herself that it was a *sign* that he *was* in the country, *was* in his office and *would* see her.

She kept her eyes peeled as she walked past the bank of snobby girls at the circular reception desk in the middle, with its sleek, wafer-thin computer terminals, and breathed a sigh of relief when she spotted a middle-aged woman striding towards her.

This must be Gabriel's secretary. Or one of them. At least the woman heading in her direction, unlike the girls at the reception desk, wasn't looking at her as though she were something dragged in by the cat after a night on the tiles.

'You're...?'

'Lucy. I'm sorry I didn't give...er...Gabriel my name, but I thought it might be nice to surprise him....' Lucy was open by nature, and subterfuge made her cheeks pinken.

'He can't allot you much time, I'm afraid. Mr Diaz is on a very tight schedule.'

Nicolette was well-versed in the sort of women her boss dated. This girl was not at all built in the same mould. Nor had Nicolette ever seen anyone quite so stunningly pretty and, judging from the clothes and the lack of make-up, quite so ignorant of her looks.

As they took the lift up to the directors' floor she made sure to keep the conversation light.

Lucy was grateful for that. She was awed and impossibly daunted by her surroundings. Every slab of marble and sheet of glass in the building breathed money and power. The employees were all decked out in designer suits and looked as though they were dashing off to very important, life-changing meetings.

In her jeans and T-shirt and flat black ballet shoes she felt as conspicuous as a bull in a china shop. She knew that people were staring as the lift disgorged them into a vast, elegant space, thickly carpeted, with a central circular sunken area in which various other besuited people were doing clever things in front of computers.

Her skin literally crawled with nerves, and her legs were so wobbly that it was a challenge to move one in front of the other.

Beyond the central atrium, a wide corridor was flanked on either side by private offices the likes of which could only, surely, be found in a company with profits to burn.

She found that she was lagging behind as Nicolette

strode briskly towards the office at the very end of the corridor. Noiseless air-conditioning meant that it was much cooler inside the building than it had been outside, and it felt positively chilly up here on the eighth floor. She clamped her teeth together to stop them from chattering.

'If you'd wait here…?'

Nicolette's smile was kindly but Lucy hardly noticed. Her pink mouth, lip gloss long since gone, had fallen open at the opulence of her surroundings. Light grey smoked glass concealed this outer office from prying eyes. The walls were white, and dominated on one side by a huge abstract painting and on the other by smoked ash doors behind which lay heaven only knew what. Another office? A wardrobe stuffed full of designer suits? A bathroom? Or maybe a torture chamber into which recalcitrant employees could be marched and taught valuable life lessons?

Nicolette's desk was bigger than the studio room in her house where Lucy did her meticulous drawings. At a push it could be converted into a dining table to seat ten.

She was staring at it, fighting the sensation that she had somehow been transported into a parallel universe, when she was told that Mr Diaz would see her now.

Lucy had thought she hadn't forgotten what Gabriel looked like. As she entered his office and the door behind her clicked softly closed she realised she actually had. The man slowly turning from the window where he had been standing, looking out, was so much taller than she remembered. She was pinned to the spot by eyes the colour of bitter chocolate. Time had done nothing to dim the staggering force of his personality—the same force she had felt the first time she had seen him, surrounded by his minions. It swept over her, strangling her vocal cords and scrambling her ability to think.

* * *

This was not what Gabriel had expected. He had expected a middle-aged harpy with a begging bowl and pictures of unfortunate children.

But this was the woman whose image he had never quite been able to eradicate from his head. She had been stunning then and she was even more stunning now—although he would have been hard pressed to put his finger on what, exactly, it was about her that held his gaze with such ferocious intensity.

Her skin was pale gold and smooth as satin, and that amazing hair, pulled back into a long plait that ran down the length of her narrow spine, had the same effect on him now as it had two years ago. Confronted by the one and only woman who had ever said no to him, Gabriel schooled his features into polite curiosity. He didn't know what she wanted, but the residue of his frustration and annoyance suddenly lifted.

'Thank you for seeing me.' Lucy hovered by the door, not having been invited to take one of the leather chairs that were ranged in front of a desk that was even bigger than the one belonging to his secretary. His silence was unnerving. It propelled her into hurried speech. 'You probably don't remember me. We met a couple of years ago. When you…ah…came to Somerset…Sims Electronics? It was one of the companies you took over…. I'm sorry. I didn't even introduce myself. Lucy…ah…Robins. I'm sorry. You won't have a clue who I am….'

Regret at her hasty decision to descend on him unannounced rushed over her, making her want to stumble back out of the door and as far away from this intimidating building as she could get. She didn't know if she should walk towards him and extend her hand in a gesture of politeness, but just the thought of touching him sent her nerves into further debilitating freefall.

Not have a clue who she was? Gabriel wanted to laugh aloud at that one. One look at her face and he was realising that her polite rejection still rankled a lot more than he had suspected. He was not a man who had his advances spurned. The experience had burnt a hole in his memory. But what the hell was she doing here? Had she turned up two years ago he would have assumed that it was because she'd had a rethink about her incomprehensible decision to turn him away—but now…? All this time later…? No, something was at play here, and intense curiosity kicked into gear. It felt great. Invigorating. Especially after his ludicrous phone call with Imogen.

'Are you going to say anything?' she asked, her nerves making her stumble over the question.

At that, Gabriel pushed himself away from the window and indicated one of the chairs in front of his desk.

'I remember you,' he drawled, resuming his seat and watching every detail of the emotions flitting across her face. 'The girl from the garden centre. You returned an item of jewellery. What did you do with the flowers? Introduce them to the incinerator?'

Lucy lowered her eyes and fumbled her way to the chair, not knowing whether he expected an answer to that deliberately provocative question. Her skin was burning, as though someone had shoved her to stand in front of an open flame, and although she wasn't looking at him the harsh, perfect angles of his face were imprinted in her head with the forcefulness of a branding iron.

Staring down uncomfortably at her entwined fingers, she literally could see nothing else but his dark-as-midnight eyes, the curl of his sensuous mouth, the coolly arrogant inclination of his head. But she was glad to be sitting. At least it gave her legs some reprieve from the threat of collapsing under her.

'So what do you want?' Gabriel asked with studied indifference. 'You have ten minutes of my time and counting.'

Lucy balled her hands into fists. She understood that they had parted company on less than ideal terms. Perhaps his pride had been wounded because she had turned him down. But was that any reason for him to make this even more difficult for her than it already was? Two years ago she had been offered a glimpse of his arrogance. Now she could see that in no way had it diminished over time.

'I've come about my father.' She took a deep breath and forced herself to meet his mildly enquiring gaze. 'I don't know if you've heard, but there's been a bit of a situation… at the company…'

Gabriel frowned. His business interests were so extensive that entire companies that sheltered under his umbrella were practically self-accounting. Now he rapidly clicked his computer and began scrolling through all the details of Sims. It took him no time at all to unearth what her mystery trip to his office was all about.

'By *situation*,' he said coldly, 'I take it that you're referring to your father's embezzlement?'

'Please don't call it that.'

'You're here because your father's been caught out with his hand in the till. I'm hoping you're not going to ask me to turn a blind eye to his thieving just because once upon a time I gave you a second look…?'

Mortification ripped through her, making her slight frame tremble. 'You don't understand! My father's not *a thief*.'

'No? Then we have a different take on what constitutes a thief. In my view, it's someone who has been caught trying to rip a company off…dipping into the coffers…taking money…' He leant forward and placed the palms of his hands flat on his desk. 'Taking money without permission, presumably to enjoy the high life!'

'He… Look, he knows that what he did was wrong….'

'Good! Then perhaps the courts will look on him favourably and not make the sentence too harsh! Alternatively, they might just want to flex their muscles and demonstrate that fraud isn't something to be taken lightly! Now…'

He stood up and cursed himself for the impact she still seemed to have on him—even when she was sitting in *his* chair, in *his* office, bleating on about her father and trying to pull the sympathy card. All of which added up to a situation with which he had less than zero tolerance.

'If that's all, Nicolette will show you out….'

CHAPTER TWO

LUCY'S SPINE STIFFENED in stubborn, angry refusal to see this as the conclusion of her expedition to London. He had treated her with contempt and hadn't even bothered to hear her out. Of course he had every good reason to dismiss her, but the thought of her father being chucked into a prison cell like a common criminal.... He would never survive that, and neither would her mother.

She could feel his eyes burning into her downturned head and she fought down the sickening wave of pride that made her want to leave with her head held high. Right now pride was a commodity she couldn't afford.

'Please...please hear me out,' she whispered, daunted beyond belief by the cold hostility emanating from him.

'Whatever for?' Gabriel's voice was harshly blunt. 'Embezzlement in my company is not accepted on any level. It's as simple as that. It's outrageous to think that you came here to parade your wares in front of me in the hope that I might bend the rules. Hell, you haven't even bothered to wear something decent!'

'Parade my wares?' Lucy looked at him with bewilderment.

'I wasn't born yesterday. I know the way women operate. Fair means or foul pretty much sums it up. You thought that you could use your sexy little body to score a few points. Big mistake. I've seen a lot of sexy bodies in my time, and I'm inured to *any* woman who tries to use hers for any kind of profit.'

Sexy little body. Those three words, uttered so casually, brought a hectic colour to her cheeks. Having never considered herself in terms of how she looked, it was somehow shocking to hear him refer to her appearance so bluntly.

She was also uncomfortable with the brief surge of pleasure she'd felt at hearing herself described as *sexy*. She had never felt like a sexy woman. Sexy women had attitude. They flashed their eyes and swayed their hips and pouted and flirted. She had never done any of those things, and wouldn't have been able to do them even if she had spent a lifetime reading books on how to achieve it. She just *wasn't* sexy, and that was why she had shied away from relationships with boys at college.

She was conservative, traditional—one of those boring types who had never slept around and was saving herself for the guy she eventually fell in love with. Her parents had done a good job in instilling values that had long been left by the wayside by most girls over the age of seventeen.

And yet he had called her *sexy*. She thought that perhaps he needed his eyes checked, but now was hardly the time to point that out. Not when he was staring at her as though she was something that had crawled out of a dustbin into his immaculate office with the sole intention of making a mess.

'I didn't come here to…to…'

Watching the rise and fall of her chest, and inwardly remarking on a repertoire of facial expressions he hadn't seen in a very long time in any woman, Gabriel caught himself wondering whether it was that wide-eyed innocence that he found so appealing. Appealing against his better judgement.

She had a face that would make any man go crazy, and yet it was coupled with a transparency that could only be dangerous.

'To…to…?' He parroted her stammer mockingly.

'You're horrible,' Lucy uttered on a desperate cry, 'and I'm really sorry I came here in the first place. I shouldn't have. Dad said that he'd tried to explain to your people at the company but none of them would listen. I might have guessed that you wouldn't listen either. I'm sorry I took up your precious time!' She began to stand up.

His order to *'Sit!'* took her so much by surprise that she practically fell back into the chair.

'You mean you're going to listen to…?'

Gabriel raised one imperious hand to cut her off mid-sentence. 'You can forget about any sob stories. Your father stole money from my company and that's the end of it. I'm not interested in listening to a long, tedious and fabricated list of extenuating circumstances. There *are* no extenuating circumstances when it comes to theft.'

He swung his long, lean body out of the chair and moved with economical grace to perch on the edge of his desk, his hands loosely clasped together. Nicolette knocked and popped into the office to remind him of a meeting due to be held in the conference room in fifteen minutes. Gabriel waved her aside.

'Let Davis cover for me,' he said, not taking his eyes off Lucy's downbent fair head. Her entire posture spoke of weary, despairing resignation. She had come to try and save her father's skin, and he supposed he could award her one or two brownie points for that, but he was pleased that she had got the essential message—which was that he was no sucker. Spinning him hard luck stories was a non-starter.

He knew that at this juncture he should send her away

and let her father try and convince the long arm of the law that it had all been a terrible mistake. But why hide from the truth? She was the one who'd got away and he still found her curiously attractive. Even dressed in clothes no woman should wear, and with a begging bowl in her hands.

His last abortive relationship with Imogen…the line of beautiful bodies and beautiful faces and easy availability… he was bored with them all. He was tired of women who simpered whenever they were with him, sick of the certain knowledge that they would all do whatever he wanted, however outrageous his request might be.

At the age of thirty-two, he found his palate was lamentably jaded. Looking at the woman in front of him made him feel as though he had been injected with youth serum. Everything about her fascinated him—from her naïveté in showing up at his office with a sob story right down to the novelty of being in the company of a woman who didn't ask *How high?* the second he told her to jump.

It was almost *challenging* to think that what he had missed first time round could now be his.

Dark, speculative eyes drifted down to the shape of her small, high breasts and his arousal was as fierce as it was sudden. She chose that very moment to raise moss-green eyes to him and he smiled a slow, satisfied smile—the smile of someone anticipating victory in a battle that had yet to commence.

'How was your trip to London?' Gabriel asked, maintaining eye contact.

'I beg your pardon?'

'Good trip? It must have been a wrench leaving the plants behind….'

'Why are you asking me these questions? I thought you were in a rush. I thought you could only spare me a few minutes. What's the point wasting the few minutes I have telling you about my trip?'

'Well, it's more worthwhile than wasting them telling me about what a sterling character your father is....'

Lucy fell silent, although he continued to stare at her. She didn't know where his weird turn in the conversation was going, but she clung to the slender hope that whilst he was talking he might still be prepared to listen. Surely he couldn't be *so* lacking in emotion that he wouldn't even hear her out?

His dark, watchful eyes set up a series of stirring reactions inside her until she could feel her temples begin to throb. She just didn't know what he wanted her to say and confusion brought a flush of colour to her cheeks. 'I...the journey was fine....'

'And your job? How's that going?'

'Good. Great. I...' She was gripped by a sudden idea and her eyes brightened. 'Better than great, in fact. I...I don't only work in the garden centre—I do quite a bit of illustrative work as well. I...I did a degree in graphic art and I was commissioned two years ago to do some drawings of the rare plants and flowers for a compendium the centre was putting together....'

Gabriel made a non-committal sound that was neither encouraging nor discouraging. Frankly he couldn't care less about whatever drawings she had been commissioned to do, but he was enjoying the genuine enthusiasm on her face. He toyed with the pleasant thought that *he* might be able to generate that same enthusiasm. Once more he was subjected to a wildly pressing urge to release her hair so that he could tangle his fingers in its rippling length.

Any woman in possession of looks like hers should not have been caught dead in a pair of faded jeans and a T-shirt—least of all in *his* presence. He had expressed disgust that she might come to him with a view to using her body to get what she wanted without even bothering to dress for the occasion, but now he realised that he would have been disappointed had she done so.

Hadn't he had his fill of Barbie dolls? Wasn't he sick to his back teeth of women who were perfectly manicured, perfectly groomed and perfectly dressed in the most expensive and revealing clothes that money could buy?

Lucy was disconcerted by that lazy appraisal in his roving dark eyes. It made her feel uncomfortable. She suppressed the crazy notion that buried beneath her discomfort a slow swirl of excitement was eddying in her veins, making her breasts tingle and sending a shooting, melting warmth between her legs.

She pressed her legs firmly together and leaned forward, gripping the soft leather of the chair. 'What I'm trying to say,' she said quickly, because he struck her as a man who lost interest fast and she needed to grab his attention before that happened, 'is that I get paid well for my art work. I've been putting money aside for the past couple of years. I've been trying to save so that I can afford to buy the little cottage I rent at the moment. Mrs Hardy, who owns it, says that she'll continue renting it to me until I can afford to put down a deposit and get a mortgage from the bank....'

'Where are you going with this?'

'Right. Well...would you be amenable to *me* paying you back the money that Dad...er...borrowed from your company? You can take all the money I've saved. It's a little over four thousand pounds. And I'm willing and happy to give you everything I earn. I mean, I'd have to keep a little aside for bills and food, but you could have the rest....'

'First, your father didn't *borrow* the money. Second, I'm afraid your savings and some of your monthly earnings wouldn't begin to put a dent in his debt. Frankly, you'd be paying me until the day you died and beyond. So you can scrap that suggestion straight away.'

'In other words there's no point to me being here at all, is there?'

Lucy watched her bright idea disappear over the horizon, taking with it all hope that she might appeal to Gabriel's better side. It was clear that he didn't have one of those. Not only that, but he was deriving great enjoyment from watching her squirm. Perhaps this was his way of exacting revenge for having been turned down by her two years ago. A man like Gabriel Diaz, blessed with drop-dead good looks and the trappings of wealth, would not be used to *any* woman turning him down. She was now paying the high price for being one of that rare breed of woman who had.

'Call me crazy—because anyone else in my situation would have thrown you out on your ear the second you walked into this office and opened your mouth—but you might have a way out of this….'

'Really?' Hope flared and she looked at him with nervous, wary anticipation.

Gabriel noted that she had amazing eyes. They were a peculiar shade of green—deep green, the colour of the sea in certain lights.

'Really. But before I get to what I have in mind let me ask you this: what happened to the boyfriend?'

'Sorry?' Lucy frowned, at a loss to understand where this reference to a boyfriend had come from. She didn't *have* a boyfriend.

'The boyfriend,' Gabriel said impatiently. 'The one you told me you had when you sent me your Dear John text.'

'I really offended you back then, didn't I?'

Gabriel laughed with caustic amusement. '*Offended* me?'

'I—I didn't mean to...' Lucy continued in an anxious stammer. 'I'm not used to...'

'Spare me the involved explanation. Just tell me the fate of the boyfriend.'

Lucy had no idea what this had to do with the matter in hand. She had to cast her mind back even to remember that small white lie. At the time the presence of a man in her life had seemed the only way of wriggling out of the situation. Gabriel Diaz had oozed sex, and there was no way she would have accepted his proposition. He had also oozed persistence. Added together, she had felt it perfectly acceptable to produce a fictitious other half, and afterwards she'd been very glad she had done so—because a quick trip on the internet had shown her what she had already suspected. Gabriel Diaz was a player—a man who, from everything she had read, worked his way through women without conscience. There were pictures of him with various beauties, none of whom had stayed the course of time.

'He...ah...it didn't work out,' Lucy mumbled, dropping her gaze and staring with furious concentration at the tips of her very unflattering black pumps.

'No? What went wrong?'

'I don't really want to talk about it,' she muttered, licking her lips and frantically trying to imagine what the fate of this made up guy might have been. One tiny and necessary white lie was one thing. A series of follow-on lies was not going to do. But his continuing silence was already telling her that she was expected to expand. And yet, she thought with a rare spark of defiance, why should she? He had been horrible to her. Arrogant, sneering and dismissive. Why should she tell him anything she didn't want to?

But that sliver of hope he had dangled in front of her was an effective gag on her rebellious thoughts. If nothing else she owed it to her parents to take advantage of any crumb of mercy he was prepared to throw her way. Perhaps he could arrange for her father to be let go, but for his reputation to remain intact and any prison sentence to be waived. That would certainly be a worthwhile result. Her parents played an active part in the community. It would be hard if her father's situation were to become public knowledge. Fortunately the two men who had uncovered the problem were both Londoners and would not be hanging around.

'He…um…broke up with me,' Lucy imparted reluctantly. 'And then, shortly afterwards, he went away. To… to New Zealand… To live with the woman he dumped me for…' This seemed the best way to ensure that her fictitious boyfriend was well and truly out of the way. 'But I still don't understand what this has to do with anything….'

'A boyfriend on the scene would have been a nuisance when it comes to what I have in mind….' Gabriel didn't *do* women with husbands, and he didn't do women who had boyfriends either. Why would he? The world was full of beautiful, single, willing women. Why go to the trouble of courting someone who came with baggage?

'And what *do* you have in mind?'

'You. I have *you* in mind.' Gabriel watched with wonderment a face that expressed absolutely no comprehension of what he was getting at.

She was literally at a loss. Any other woman would have followed the thread of this conversation, and certainly by now would have got the message loud and clear. This woman was staring at him with a frown, as though he had produced a complicated maths problem from under a hat and demanded she provide a solution immediately.

'May I do something?' he asked with silken assurance, and then, just in case she was *still* away with the fairies and not getting where he was going, he strolled behind her. Before she could react he was pulling free her hair, releasing it from its constricting braid.

Lucy swivelled round and stood up, faltering backwards until she bumped into the edge of his desk.

'What are you doing?' With one hand she clasped her loosed hair, pulling it over one shoulder. She couldn't peel her eyes away from his face, and her heart was pounding so fiercely in her chest that she could scarcely breathe. She gave a little squeak of horror as he very slowly strolled towards her.

'I wanted to do that the first time I laid eyes on you,' Gabriel murmured.

He smiled, and that smile had the effect of making her feel as though she was falling through the air with no safety net beneath her. Her stomach lurched and every nerve in her body was at screaming pitch.

'I saw you on that bike and I wanted you. Simple as that. You were like a gazelle—all beauty and grace. And, mysteriously, I find that I *still* want you….'

'But you *can't*…' Lucy breathed jerkily. 'You…you date supermodels….'

'How do you know that?'

'Because I looked you up on the internet!' She went bright red. He was standing so close to her that she could feel his heat. He must be able to feel hers, because she was certainly burning up.

'You did, did you?' Gabriel was intensely satisfied that he had made more of an impression on her than he had given himself credit for—boyfriend or no boyfriend. An indifferent woman would never have looked him up on the internet. More to the point, an indifferent woman wouldn't be looking at him now with lurking excitement in her eyes. Even if she *was* strenuously trying to conceal it. An expert when it came to the opposite sex, he could sense her response to him as clearly as if it had been emblazoned on her forehead in neon lettering.

'I was curious….' Lucy defended.

'Curiosity is good.' He leant forward to brace himself on the desk, his hands on either side of her, caging her in.

The fantasy of taking her here—in his office, on his desk—was so powerful that he hardened, his erection painful as it pressed thickly against the zipper of his trousers. Gone was the jaded, world-weary feeling that had settled over him for what seemed like years. For that alone she would be worth every penny.

'So here's my proposal…'

Regretfully, he straightened, because being so close to her, breathing in that refreshing innocence, the clean, minty smell of her fabulous hair, was doing all sorts of things to his body. Much as he enjoyed the sensation, he had to acknowledge that they *were* in his office, and Nicolette *was* just one door away. Having his secretary accidentally burst in on a scene of rampant lovemaking on his desk would not be good for her dodgy blood pressure.

At no point did it occur to him that Lucy might reject his advances the way she had rejected them two years ago. This time he held the trump card, and he had every intention of using it.

As he strolled back towards his chair he could feel her eyes on him, and he knew with every primitive instinct in his body that she had not been immune to that brief moment of contact when he had touched her hair.

'I won't try to wrap it up in any fancy packaging. I want you, and in return for having you in my bed I'm willing to let your father off the hook. All the stolen money will be replaced. Orders issued to my two finance guys that with the debt owing to me cleared the matter is to be buried, never again to resurface. Of course your father won't be able to return to his job. That would be taking the joke a step too far. After all, a thief is a thief is a thief. But he will be retired with a generous package, and hopefully a salutary lesson in never dipping his fingers in the till of any company again....'

Lucy couldn't help staring at him. Here was the same man who had shown up at the garden centre with his lackeys in tow and a dinner invitation he'd expected to be accepted. Now he was offering her an invitation of another sort, and this time he was calling the shots. She was truly appalled at his lack of morality. Was this how *all* rich people operated? Did they assume that they just needed to snap their fingers and the rest of the world would dance to their tune?

'That's ridiculous...' She edged away from the desk and began backing unsteadily towards the door. She eyed the backpack she had brought with her. It was on the ground, next to the chair she had fallen into when she had first entered his office. Her unravelled hair fell in a long, thick blond curtain over one shoulder, but she was hardly aware of it as she took small steps towards the bag.

'What's so ridiculous about it?'

His words halted her, and she jerked up to stare at him with an expression of disbelief. 'You're asking me to be... to...'

'Sleep with me...make love...have sex—at times and places of my choosing... No need to tiptoe over the details.'

'But that's utterly immoral!'

'So's stealing—and on the plus side sex *isn't* a criminal offence punishable with a jail sentence....' He was incredulous that she was even quibbling over his generous offer. As rescue packages went, he didn't think she could have landed herself a better one.

And yet she was still staring at him as though he had

asked if she wouldn't mind stripping off and running naked down the street. What exactly, he wondered, was the problem here? If she was playing hard to get in an attempt to up the ante then she was definitely barking up the wrong tree. He would never have dreamt of doing a deal like this with any other woman. Perhaps that had something to do with the fact that she was the only woman ever to have turned him down. But, although she might be the exception, her window of opportunity was small.

'I'm sorry. I couldn't.'

Lucy retrieved her backpack and clutched it in front of her like a shield. She wondered whether there was anything else she could say that would buy her father some clemency, but in her heart she knew that the offer on the table was the only one this man would be making. She also knew that by turning it down she was condemning her parent to swift retribution.

But how could she possibly do what he wanted? Sex, for him, was clearly no more than a physical transaction. It was irrelevant that there was no emotion involved. She had always promised herself that sex for her would have lots of emotion involved. How could she abandon the moral principles she had been weaned on?

Gabriel shrugged. He strolled towards her and received the impression that she was holding her ground only by the skin of her teeth. Given half a chance she would have hightailed it through the door at speed.

'Your choice,' he told her with casual indifference.

'Isn't there something else you want?' Lucy asked desperately.

'No.' Gabriel refused to mince words. 'That's the only deal on the table.'

'And so…my dad…'

'Goodbye freedom. Hello Cell Block H…'

'You're the most heartless, unsympathetic man I've ever met in my entire life!'

'But I have many other things to offer….' Gabriel's voice was low and husky. She had a dusting of freckles on her nose and her eyelashes were so thick and dark that anyone would think she had laid on the mascara with a trowel were it not for the fact that she radiated a natural glow that had nothing to do with make-up.

He had always found that a certain element of surprise worked when it came to disarming his opponents. He used it now.

Lucy, staring at him with the dazed expression of someone suddenly subjected to a whiplash rollercoaster of events they had been least expecting, was not prepared for his lean brown hand as he reached to curl his fingers in her hair. She was certainly not prepared for his cool mouth as it descended to meet hers, and she was even less prepared for the way her body was galvanised into a reaction that was so strong it deprived her of the ability to breathe.

She had been kissed before, but never like this. As his tongue gently parted her lips she felt scorching heat race through her. Her breasts were heavy, sensitive to the slight brush of his chest against hers. Her nipples tingled in a way that shot signals to every other part of her body. Like wax subjected to open flame, she was melting. She heard a low moan and was shocked to realise that it was coming from *her*.

With a push, she separated her treacherous body from his and found no opposition. Indeed, he released her immediately and stood back with a slight smile curving his beautiful mouth.

'How *could* you?'

'Take advantage of you? You enjoyed it…'

'I did *not*!' Lucy cried fiercely. 'I'm *not* like that! I'm *not* like those women you go out with!' But she was mortified, and ashamed of her body—which was loudly protesting her virtuous words. 'I'm going!'

She took a couple of panicky steps to remove herself from the stranglehold of his proximity and he didn't follow her. He reached for something on his desk, scribbled on it.

'Here's my card. I'll give you twenty-four hours, and after that my offer expires. Word of advice? It's a generous offer. Think very carefully before you decide to put your principles ahead of common sense. And don't kid yourself that you would be disgusted by the deal. You came alive for me just then, and there's plenty more where that came from....'

'Don't *say* those things!' But already she was reacting to his words, her mind flashing erotic images through her head—images that made her squirm because they were so new, so unexpected, so horribly, frighteningly different from anything she had ever experienced before.

She was barely aware of leaving his office. She couldn't have said how she managed to make it to the train station or get on the train. Several times she looked at the card he had given her and was tempted to rip it into shreds and chuck it in the nearest bin.

So why didn't she? He had offered her a devil's contract. She should have thrown that card away the second she left his office. She should never have accepted it in the first place!

Her thoughts were all over the place. Scenery flashed past and she saw none of it. When she tried to recall the conversation they had had all she could see was his sinfully handsome face, all she could hear was the velvety persuasiveness of his low, sexy drawl. He hadn't touched her, but she felt as though he had. Her body tingled as though he had run those lean brown fingers over it.

She was determined that he couldn't *buy* her, but even as she stood self-righteously on her podium and declared that as an absolute certainty a little voice in her head was reminding her of how he had made her feel, how that kiss had cut through all her fine words and blown them apart into smithereens.

Once home, she briefly dropped in to make sure Freddy was all right, and then drove to her parents' house—to find neither of them there and the house in darkness.

On top of everything that had been going on this could only mean bad news—which was confirmed when she called her father on his mobile to be told that they were at the hospital.

'Your mother had a turn.'

He was holding it together, but with difficulty. Lucy could hear that down the phone line.

'I didn't want to worry you. You've been worried enough already. At any rate, they're doing tests, but they think she may have had a mild panic attack. They'll keep her in overnight. There's no need to get yourself into a tizzy about it….'

But that was easier said than done.

In the space of a couple of days her world had shifted on its axis. Her comfortable routine had been blown apart.

At the hospital, exhausted after a day's worth of travelling, Lucy was cheered to hear that her mother had indeed suffered only a mild panic attack, but when the doctor took her aside, with her father, and gravely told them that they should make sure that Celia was kept as stress-free as possible, she could only think of that offer Gabriel had made.

What price high-minded principles when her mother was lying on a hospital bed and her father was staring down the barrel of a gun?

Would it be the end of the world for *her*? Was she *re-*

ally prepared to sacrifice her parents for the wonderful prize of her virginity?

It was dark by the time she eventually made it back to her cottage. After a day cooped up indoors Freddy was raring for some fun and she spent half an hour outside with him. Her mind was clouded with anxiety as she threw his ball and watched as he fetched it, romping back to her triumphantly and waiting so that the exercise could be repeated.

Lucy knew what she had to do, but it wasn't going to be easy.

And yet the memory of that searing kiss leapt into her head and her heart began to pound.

The palms of her hands were clammy when, an hour later, after she had tried and failed to have something to eat, she tapped Gabriel's number into her telephone.

The business card he had given her displayed a dizzying array of numbers but he had handwritten his cell number, which probably meant that it was a number only released to a small number of privileged people. She figured that the women who had that number probably thought they had won the lottery.

He picked up on the third ring and immediately she wondered where he was. At the office? In his house or apartment, or whatever expensive pad he called home? It certainly wouldn't be a quaint little house in the suburbs!

'It's me. It's Lucy. Lucy Robins. I came to see you at your off—'

'My memory is in perfect working order,' Gabriel said drily. He had literally just stepped through the front door of his sprawling house in Kensington. It was the one of the most prestigious houses in one of the most prestigious roads in London.

He began removing his tie, heading to the kitchen to

pour himself a whisky. Amazing. Even the sound of her voice had an invigorating effect on his libido.

'I'm taking it you've had a little think about the conversation we had today…?' he encouraged, when her awkward, stammering introduction was followed by complete silence.

'Yes, I have.'

'And you've come to what conclusion? That your father is to face those cruel, unforgiving and heartless scales of justice and reap his due rewards?'

'No…'

That single monosyllable sounded as though it had been dragged out of her, but Gabriel was unperturbed by that. Had she really been as repulsed by him as she had tried to convince him then the offer would have been withdrawn. But she wasn't. Reaching for a glass, he smiled to himself—the satisfied smile of a predator that has successfully corralled its prey and can look forward to enjoying the catch.

'Maybe we can talk,' she muttered.

'Count on it. I'll be with you tomorrow.' Some meetings would have to be rearranged, but she was a prize that would be worth that small inconvenience.

'No!' Lucy was alone in the cottage, but she still looked guiltily around her—as though at any moment the walls might decide to spout ears. Have Gabriel swan down to Somerset? She could think of nothing worse! There was no way she would ever let her parents suspect that she had struck this deal. They would be horrified. It would be her shameful secret and would have to be kept exclusively in London. A shameful weekend secret. It was the only way. 'I…I can come to London at the weekend…'

'Not sure I can wait that long.'

'Please. It's only two days away. If you give me your

address…or better still we could meet at…a restaurant…or something…'

'I'll text you my address.' Anticipation roared through him as it never had before. 'When I see you I don't want anyone around.' He was already thinking of that slender, loose-limbed body, as graceful as a dancer's. He would definitely have to have a cold shower tonight. 'I can't wait….'

CHAPTER THREE

TWO DAYS LATER Lucy was back on the train, speeding up to London. On the one hand she was a nervous wreck. Gabriel was no longer someone she could shove to the back of her mind and forget because he wasn't physically around.

He had phoned her twice since her decision to give him what he wanted. She felt as if he was keeping tabs on her, making sure his quarry wasn't allowed any second thoughts, although his conversations were not at all threatening. He asked her about her day and expressed interest in the details. Lucy didn't believe for a minute that he really cared one way or the other about successfully transplanted orchids or the large order the garden centre had taken from a chain of hotels in the north. She knew that he was trying to put her at her ease, but instead of feeling relieved she just felt increasingly as if she had been bought and was now being primed for consumption.

On the other hand the wheels were in motion for her father's reprieve.

She had told her dad haltingly, because lying didn't come easy—especially lying to her parent—that she had managed to get in touch with Gabriel and the meeting had been a good one.

'I think he might be prepared to let you off,' she had said only the morning before.

A more suspicious parent would have immediately jumped to the right conclusion that any favour granted from someone like Gabriel Diaz would require a hefty payback, but suspicion didn't run deep in Nicholas Robins's bones. He was a man who saw the good in people, and he had had no trouble accepting that Gabriel Diaz had been open to persuasion.

'It's a first-time offence,' she had offered by way of explanation for a decision that made no sense, 'and I don't know—maybe he doesn't want to get on the wrong side of the local people by dragging you through the courts. I…er…told him how sorry you were, and how affected everyone in the community would be if you were to be punished…how they close ranks against outsiders…'

'And did you tell him that I will be willing to sacrifice all my pay until the debt's cleared? I could get a second job…something to bring a little money in… The bulk of my earnings could go towards paying him back…. Did you mention that I had already started making repayments?'

Lucy hadn't had the heart to tell her father that the likelihood of him returning to his old job was about as likely as a trip to the moon. Instead she had waxed lyrical about Gabriel's wonderfully sympathetic nature…the vast reserves of wealth that had enabled him to write off her father's debt as a mere bagatelle that could be swept under the carpet…his empathy for a man who had borrowed money, misguidedly, for a very worthwhile cause…

She'd had to stop herself from laughing out loud at the one hundred percent inaccurate and ridiculous picture she had painted of a man who was just the opposite of the one she had so feverishly described to her father.

The main thing was that her father no longer faced the threat of being thrown into prison. Also, her mother had been released from the hospital and was cheered by this change in their fortunes.

They were both so naive that Lucy could have wept, but she'd kept up the optimistic front and only sagged when she'd got to the station and bade farewell to her village for the weekend.

Details to finalise, she had told them, and then, to add credence to her story, she had hinted that she liked Gabriel more than she was letting on.

All in all she had given an award-winning performance. She hated herself for it, but her hands were tied.

Now she stared down at the overnight bag that was on the seat next to her. She was travelling first class at Gabriel's insistence. Well, it was preferable to the car he had offered to send for her, or the helicopter that he'd assured her would be no great trouble. She had explained a lot to her parents, but there was no way she could have explained a helicopter landing in the village square to collect her.

As soon as her eyes alighted on the overnight bag her pulses began to race and she had to lean back and briefly close her eyes. Tonight she should have been going to the movies with two of her girlfriends, who had now also been on the receiving end of a few white lies. Her life, which had been so uncomplicated before, now seemed to be comprised of a string of half-truths. She was an innocent little insect that had inadvertently strayed into a spider's web, and her every move ensured greater entrapment.

Gabriel had told her that a driver would be sent to collect her from the station. But she walked out into the blinding sunshine to see immediately that any prolonged period of reprieve was at an end—because Gabriel himself was there, casually dressed and looking ludicrously out of place amidst the banks of stressed-out, tired passengers leaving the station.

She couldn't fail to notice how many women looked at him. He, with arrogant indifference, appeared not to notice the attention he was getting. He was lounging against the railings, his eyes hidden behind dark sunglasses. Across the street she could see his black limo, parked and waiting.

Gabriel spotted her as soon as she walked out of the station and noted with dissatisfaction that she seemed to have gone to great pains to dress in the least flattering outfit conceivable. Not jeans this time, but combat trousers the colour of sludge and yet another T-shirt. The flat shoes had been replaced with trainers. He didn't think that he had ever gone out with or even personally known *any* woman who possessed a pair of trainers. As far as he was concerned that kind of footwear was suitable only for the gym.

Even disadvantaged by her poor choice of clothing, though, her beauty was still a source of radiance. Her impossibly long hair was back in its habitual braid, and once more his fingers itched to undo it. He smiled in pleasant anticipation of that event and headed in her direction.

Watching him approach, his body language a textbook lesson in cool self-assurance, Lucy resisted the temptation to turn tail and flee. He was truly breathtakingly sexy, and the closer he got to her the more he took her breath away.

The enormity of what lay ahead made her want to faint, but she kept moving forward, propelled by the meaning of the relief on her parents' faces when she had told them that their troubles might be over.

'Good trip?' Gabriel relieved her of her overnight bag and wondered whether it would be rude to ferry her immediately to Harrods so that everything she possessed—overnight bag included—could be replaced. He felt he might enjoy a ceremonial burning of her entire wardrobe.

'I didn't think you would be here to meet me. You said you'd be sending your driver….'

'I found that I couldn't wait.... You should be flattered.'

Lucy was making sure not to walk too close to him. She didn't want to be here at all, had been put in a position of having no choice, and she hated the strange effect he had on her. She would be facing bigger problems soon enough. Her nervous system deserved as much rest as it could get before those problems arose.

'Where are we going now?' she asked anxiously, stepping back as he opened the door of the car for her.

'I expect you're in need of a bath.' Gabriel waited until he was sitting next to her before he went on. 'Train journeys always have that effect on me.'

'Do you take many?'

She pressed herself against the door and Gabriel suppressed a stab of sheer annoyance. This wasn't what he was used to. Women didn't act disappointed when they saw him, and they didn't try to put distance between them. It was going to be a challenging weekend if she intended to scuttle around him like a terrified rabbit. He cheered up when he reminded himself that he had never been one to shy away from a challenge.

'Admittedly, no,' Gabriel conceded with an elegant shrug. 'I don't do delays, timetables or discomfort. We'll be going back to my place. You can have a bath. Freshen up...'

Lucy didn't want to dwell on any of those disconcerting things and rushed into hasty speech. 'I want to thank you for calling your people off Dad. He said that he's been told by them that charges aren't going to be pressed and he's very relieved.'

'I'm sure he is,' Gabriel responded smoothly. 'I would be, too, were I in his position. There can be nothing so worrying as a trip to a police station followed by a prison sentence. How did he take our little deal? I suppose, given the alternative, he wasn't overly bothered….'

'I didn't go into the details.' Lucy shot him a look of simmering resentment from under her lashes.

'That must have been difficult, given the circumstances. How many employers would have consent to overlook fraud?'

'I wish you'd stop calling it that.'

'If the cap fits… So, tell me how you managed to explain the terms of our arrangement…?'

Lucy guiltily thought of the way she had tiptoed around any difficult explanation through a mixture of practically turning Gabriel into some sort of earthly saint, filled with the milk of human kindness, and implying that she was girlishly attracted to him, thereby excusing any trips to London, should this crazy situation go past a single weekend.

'I…er…they were just so pleased that…er…'

'Getting the picture. Neither of them wanted to ask too many questions. Sometimes it's easier for people to skim over the details—especially when those details might force them to take a stand. I don't like you tying your hair back like that.'

'Sorry?'

'And I'm not entirely taken with your choice of clothing either….'

'These are the kind of clothes I wear….'

'And that's great when you're surrounded by plants, mud and soil, but when you're with me the surroundings will be vastly different and you'll be expected to look the part.'

'I've been meaning to have a little chat with you about… about that…' Lucy had never been so insulted before. Nor was she turned on by the prospect of being moulded into someone who *looked the part.* But staging an argument in her defence would require a lot of tact, because the inescapable truth *was* that he had bought her. And now he presumed that he had rights.

'About what?'

'This arrangement...how long do you think it's going to take?'

Once again Gabriel fought down his annoyance. Her dewy smooth skin, light gold from time spent outdoors in the summer months, was flushed. She looked like someone who, knowing that they had to stomach a dose of vile medicine, was keen to ascertain how much, *exactly*, they would be required to swallow. Did she have any idea of how insulting her evident reluctance was?

'How long is a piece of string?' He threw the unanswerable question back at her. 'And what makes you think,' he drawled, 'that you're going to be in a hurry for it to end?'

'Of course I am! I don't even want to *be* here. I'm only here because I have no choice! Why would I want this situation to last longer than necessary?'

'I can think of one or two scenarios...'

'That's because you're egotistical and you're accustomed to women fawning over you and wanting to be in your company!' She almost wept in frustration at the slow smile he gave her. She modulated her voice and tried to infuse calm into her overwrought body. 'I'm just asking because I can't keep taking weekends off. For starters I have a dog, and I can't fob him off on Mum and Dad every weekend. They're old. They don't want the responsibility. Plus I have friends, *a life*....'

'Too bad.' There was no point humouring her on this score, Gabriel reasoned. He wondered what this *life* that she was talking about consisted of. There was no boyfriend on the scene. Or was there? Had she said what she had wanted him to hear to save her skin? Or rather the skin of her parents? 'What's this *life* you're talking about?'

'Friends…'

'Any in particular? The boyfriend from two years ago may be happily shearing sheep in New Zealand, but I'm not going to be impressed if he's been replaced by someone else and you've diplomatically decided to keep him under wraps….'

Lucy wondered how many lies she had told so far. She was losing count. Very soon she would need a calculator to keep abreast.

'I'm referring to my girlfriends. We have an active social life back home.'

'Doing what?'

'Cinema…and we have supper at each other's houses… I just need to have some sort of idea of when my life will get back to normal!'

'I think it's best to work on the assumption that "normal" for you stopped the day your father got caught stealing from me,' Gabriel remarked drily.

Without her even noticing they had left the crowded streets around the station behind and were now in an exclusive residential area. For several long minutes she could only stare at the massive elegant houses set in a street unlike any she had ever seen in all her trips to London. There were no inconvenient pedestrians cluttering the pavements, no cars bumper to bumper, impatient to get to destinations unknown. These houses were clearly owned by people wealthy enough to ensure that serenity in the middle of one of the most vibrant cities in the world was guaranteed.

When his limo pulled up in front of the most impressive of the lot—a huge, white-fronted Georgian mansion nestled at the end of a peaceful, tree-lined street that ended in a cul-de-sac—it took Lucy a while to collect her thoughts and respond to the door that was being held open for her by his driver.

There surely could not have been a more effective way of underlining what he had said about her normal life being temporarily on hold.

No wonder he had made such a song and dance about her clothes! No wonder he had told her that in his world she would have to *look the part*! She felt as though she had gone from being in *Little House on the Prairie* to *Dallas*.

Her mouth went dry as they entered the mansion. There was a lot of marble. Cream marble shot with very pale pink on which sat silk rugs in muted colours with elaborate patterns. The paintings on the walls all looked vaguely familiar. If she didn't recognise some of them, she felt she ought to.

The door shut behind her and Lucy fell back in sheer terror.

'I don't belong here,' she said quickly, staring around and clutching her backpack in both her hands.

'Interestingly, that's not the reaction my house usually generates in women.'

Gabriel moved to stand in front of her with an amused expression softening the harsh contours of his face. Lucy stared up at him, her eyes huge and round.

'Generally speaking,' he expanded, shoving his hands in his pockets and grinning, 'there's a lot of *wow...what an incredible place...I can't believe this...*'

Lucy was held captive by that grin. There was so much unconscious charm in it that she felt she could understand why women fell at his feet. Naturally she was at pains to remind herself she was immune to anything like that, given the horror of the situation in which she found herself, but still…

'Why do you need something as big as this when there's only one of you…?' she asked inanely.

He seemed to find that even more hilarious.

'I don't need to. I choose to. There's a difference.'

The tone of his voice said it all. He was a man who got what he wanted. He might not *need* something, but if he *wanted* it then he got it. He didn't *need* her, but he *wanted* her—and he had found at his disposal the perfect means to achieve that. She was a commodity that he had procured through blackmail.

'You're spoiled rotten—do you know that?' she said, turning away and fumbling with her backpack, because a sudden wave of self-pity was bringing tears to her eyes and she would not allow herself to cry about this predicament.

'Come again?'

'You're like a *kid*!' Lucy shouted, staring him down. 'An over-indulged rich kid who points his finger and knows that he can have whatever he points at—even if it's not necessary, even if the thing he wants now, *right now*, will probably be tossed aside in a day's time!'

Gabriel was enraged that she should dare to say something like that to him. But her slender frame was trembling, and if she weren't clutching her backpack she would almost certainly have been throwing it at him. And all because he had thrown her thieving father a lifeline and brought her back to a house that had twice received offers to be placed in a glossy magazine!

'You've got me here! And you won't even have the decency to tell me when I'll be released!' she practically sobbed.

Gabriel fought to control his spiralling temper. He had never been a man to lose control. He also hated hysterics.

'I'll show you to the bathroom,' he gritted.

Lucy continued to look at him with unalloyed hostility.

Her hair was unravelling from its braid and her sea-green eyes were spitting fire. How was it that she was still managing to get to him? On the one hand there was a gentleness to her that was almost childlike. On the other he had never been in the presence of such a little hellcat in his life before. Her every emotion was swept to the surface and emerged undiluted by artifice. Was that why she had such an effect on him? Because she was so incredibly different from all the other women he had been with?

He spun round and began heading up the stairs. Lucy, for want of any other option, began following him. Her backpack was slung over one shoulder. Ahead, he was carrying her overnight bag.

The majestic staircase opened onto an exquisite landing. Here, the marble gave way to rich wooden flooring, and as they passed room after room she was privy to the sight of shutters, billowing voile, deep, rich drapes and yet more of those amazing silk rugs that were to be found on the ground floor.

He turned left and she almost collided into the back of him as she came to an abrupt halt in a bedroom. Like everything else in the house the scale of this room was eye-wateringly grand. Two enormous windows overlooked a large garden and they were dressed with deep burgundy drapes. The furniture was built in, so there were no bits of furniture to interrupt the open sweep of the room or to distract the attention from the massive, aggressively masculine bed that now stared at her with mocking triumph.

Lucy croaked and stared back at it. *His room.* The room she would be sharing. With him. The bed was big, but not so big that she would be able to partition herself away from his daunting body.

She wouldn't think about that yet. She would cross that bridge when she came to it.

'Is this the room I'll be sleeping in?' she asked, on the off-chance that this was a spare bedroom—one that coincidentally looked lived-in. By him.

'I'll run you a bath.'

Gabriel pushed open a concealed door and Lucy followed him towards a bathroom that was as big as the ground floor of her cottage. The bath was huge. To Lucy's dazed eyes it looked as though it could hold a football team. Big, fluffy towels hung on a heated towel rail and she stared at him as her mouth went dry.

'Thank you,' she squeaked. 'I can take things from here.'

'Relax,' Gabriel urged. 'Admittedly these circumstances are a bit on the unusual side, but let's not kid ourselves. We're attracted to one another. There's no reason why we shouldn't have fun....'

He curved his hand to the side of her head and Lucy stopped breathing altogether as he began stroking her face, running his thumb along her cheekbone.

'I'm *not* attracted to you. You've got it all wrong....'

Her voice faltered as he ran his thumb over her mouth. Of their own accord her lips parted and she found that she could barely catch her breath. Her breasts swelled, became sensitive. She was scarcely aware of him undoing her hair, and she was even less aware of him propelling her gently back until she was against the cool tiled wall.

'Don't talk,' Gabriel murmured. He slipped his hand under her T-shirt and those dangerously long, lean fingers travelled upwards until they found the soft cotton of her bra.

Lucy had felt nothing like this in her life before. She wasn't a prude. At college there had been boys interested in her. She had even gone out with two of them. But neither had tempted her beyond the stage of kissing and some fondling.

How did any of this make sense? her mind was screaming. How had those two boys at college she had really liked not been able to get past the starting post and yet Gabriel Diaz—a man she *disliked*, a man who had *blackmailed* her into his bedroom—was now having this electrifying effect on her, sending her body into terrifying, excited freefall?

When he unclasped her bra she moaned, and she moaned more as his big hand cupped her breast, as his fingers played with her erect nipple.

Gabriel felt the conflict in her. Her face was flushed, her eyes half closed. God, her body was setting him on fire. He was so aroused that it was painful. He pushed up the T-shirt and groaned in appreciation of her small breasts, their nipples two big, rosy discs, begging to be sucked.

He had never been one to lose control when it came to sex. However beautiful and desirable a woman, he had always been able to wait. Having sex up against a wall was for horny teenagers with libidos that needed to be brought into line.

God, where was his formidable self-control now? He hoisted her up in one easy movement, marvelling at how light she was, and there her nipples were, where they should be—by his mouth.

She straddled him, her arms loosely linked behind his head and her body as hot as a piece of toast. He blindly sought out those tempting peaks, clamping his mouth over one and suckling hard so that she was gasping and wriggling and moaning in his arms.

Crazy with sensation, and barely able to get her head round what was happening, Lucy was lost. The T-shirt had completely ridden up, as had her unclasped bra, and the sight of his dark head at her breasts was an amazing turn-on. Her body was alive. It had never felt so alive. Her jeans were a cumbersome hindrance that she wanted to kick off. Her underwear, the same sensible cotton as the bra, was damp, and through her jeans the pressure of his body between her legs was sending delicate but insistent shivers through her. She had an urgent need to move against him, harder and harder, until those shivers picked up pace.

She arched back and her eyes opened, looking past his head.

In a mirror that dominated the sand-coloured tiles on the wall opposite the face that stared back at her was a face she didn't recognise. Long blond hair hung in a tangled mane over her shoulders, her lips were swollen, her skin was flushed, as though she was in the grip of a terrible fever, and her eyes glittered with an excitement she had never seen in them in her life before.

It was a truly terrifying sight, and she began wriggling to be put down.

'Wha—?'

'Put me down! What are you *doing*?'

'What am *I* doing?'

It took a few seconds for her protests to get through to him. As soon as she was out of his arms she wrenched down the T-shirt and glared at him.

'You...you...' Lucy spluttered, and tried to think of some fitting put-down. But all she could see in her mind's eye was that disturbing vision of herself in the mirror. 'I want you to leave this bathroom *immediately*!'

'Stop playing games.' Gabriel caught her hand, forcing her to look up at him with glaring accusation. 'And stop kidding yourself that you want me to leave you alone.'

'I *do* want you to leave me alone! I'm not happy to be here and the last thing I need is for you to...to...think that you can just...*assault* me!'

'Be *very* careful how you use your words....'

Lucy stared at him mutely. She didn't understand what was going on. Her heart was thumping so hard she could feel it banging against her ribcage and her body was still throbbing from where it had been touched.

'This isn't me,' she whispered. 'I know what you want from me, but I'm not that kind of person....'

'You don't *think* you are.' He dropped her hand and stood back. 'I'll be waiting in the bedroom for you.'

Gabriel spun round on his heels and heard her lock the door behind him. *Assault?* Her use of that word was highly incendiary, and he was outraged that she could throw herself into the role of victim when not only was he doing her a favour but she had come to him with a smile on her face and a body that was giving off all the right signals.

His arousal was taking a long time to subside. He flung himself on the bed and watched the closed bathroom door with scowling intensity, waiting for it to open and giving himself time to cool down.

This was *not* the sort of situation he had envisaged. When he had tendered his offer he had imagined that she would be relieved—grateful and eager to do whatever he wanted. He had sidestepped her professed hesitation, barely giving it the time of day because he had known underneath all the wide eyes and the um-ing and ah-ing that she found him attractive. He had looked forward to a relationship in which there was mutual understanding and no unreasonable expectations of a happy-ever-after. They would have sex, and it would be an arrangement in which there would be profit on both sides.

For her, her father would walk free. For him, he would finally net the one woman who had escaped him, and the terms would not involve any fear on his part of her wanting any more than she was going to get.

He would never conceive of actually *buying* any woman. Why would he? But in this one instance he had been prepared to make an exception—and how was she reacting? With a ridiculous temper tantrum, insults, and a locked bathroom door. It made no sense to him. He was tempted to break down the door and physically show her just how self-deluded she was in imagining that her response just then had been the response of a woman who didn't want to be where she was. But breaking down bathroom doors would be taking things several steps too far.

He was beginning to rethink that decision when she eventually emerged, draped in his dressing gown that had been hanging on a hook behind the bathroom door. It swamped her. She had tried to keep her hair dry, but damp tendrils hung over her shoulders.

'My bag is on the bed,' Lucy muttered, going hot and cold and averting her eyes from the sight of him splayed with masculine abandon on the giant bed.

'If you're thinking of another pair of jeans, or more of those hideous trousers you were wearing earlier, then you might as well forget it.'

Quick as that, he had forgotten the foul mood into which he had been plunged by her incomprehensible behaviour. She looked good enough to eat, but he was going to make sure that she came to him now. *Begging.* Her pupils were dilated and her trembling hesitancy spoke volumes about a woman who was scared to get too close just in case she went up in flames again.

He liked the thought of being the man who could incite such contradictory responses in her. She could bare her claws all she wanted, and rant and rail about his terrible behaviour in taking advantage of the perilous situation with her father—but, hell, she *still* wanted him…she *still* couldn't help herself.

He felt himself stir as he continued to gaze at her rosy-cheeked face. He patted the space on the bed next to him and smiled.

'I want to get changed.'

'Feel free.' Gabriel relaxed a little more, folded his hands behind his head and followed with interest her reluctance to take him up on his offer.

Her bag was next to him. Lucy tentatively approached it, but as she was about to reach for it he got to her first and pulled her down towards him.

The robe fell open as she flopped on the bed next to him and he hissed long and low under his breath at the sight of those succulent little breasts with their rosy tips. His mind was galvanised into such graphic images that he clenched his jaw to stave off his erection getting out of hand.

There was a lot to be said for variety, he was discovering. His palate was a lot more jaded than he had originally thought!

'Gabriel…no!' Lucy scuttled away from him and clutched the robe around her tightly.

Gabriel sat up. 'I don't go for women who play games.'

'I'm *not* playing games. I *know* why I'm here. I *know* we have a deal and my half of the bargain is to…is to…'

'Lucy, it's no use coming over all girlish and pretending that I'm forcing you to do something you don't want to do.' Gabriel was determined to drag her kicking and screaming towards reality if it killed him. 'And I'm not going to be accused of *assaulting* you.'

'I'm sorry. It was wrong of me to say that.' Much as she might want to stick to that handy description, which would absolve her of all culpability in what had happened earlier in the bathroom, driving honesty compelled her to tell the truth—at least on that front. She closed her eyes briefly and drew in a deep, stabilising breath.

'Ah. So we're inching our way towards an understanding of what's going on here, are we? Slowly but surely you're beginning to wake up to the fact that our trade-off isn't the nightmare you keep telling yourself it is….'

He vaulted off the bed and paced the room. Lucy followed his prowling progress with feverish eyes. He dragged a stool from the window to the bed and settled on it.

'For as long as we're in a relationship you'll enjoy the fruits of my money, and it's not going to be torture. You're burning up for me—so get over your conscience and relax and enjoy what's on the table. You won't even be at my beck and call. You work with your plants during the week and I make sure that my weekends are kept free for you and you alone…suits me down to the ground…'

'I can't give you what you want….'

'You're already giving it to me. I haven't been so turned on by a woman in years…. In fact, I can't remember the last time I wanted to have a woman the second I laid eyes on her—but that's what you do to me. I took one look at you at the station and I would have had you in the back seat of my car if the windows had been blacked out…'

'You're just turned on because I didn't fall at your feet!'

'Who cares about the whys and wherefores?'

'*You* will. Because I'm a virgin….'

CHAPTER FOUR

GABRIEL LOOKED AT her for a few silent seconds, then he burst out laughing.

'Give me a break! Who are you trying to kid? And what leverage do you think a lie like that will give you? You've already got me to settle your father's debt...and I've already told you that while you're with me, you'll enjoy all the things money can buy...so why hold out for further prizes by telling me that you're a virgin?'

Lucy stared furiously at his smirking face. His entire speech made her feel cheap, but there was nothing else she could expect. Nor could she labour the point about it being hateful—not when she had willingly allowed him to touch her; not when her body had responded to that touch with the speed of dry tinder combusting.

'I'm not kidding.'

Gabriel's laughter died in his throat. His eyes skimmed her mutinous closed face and took in the earnestness of her expression. It was beyond belief, but *could* she be telling the truth?

'Of course you are. You're in your twenties...'

'I'm twenty-four—and don't tell me that I'm not telling the truth!' She shied away from the open incredulity in those fabulous, knowing dark eyes. She couldn't have picked a less worthy recipient of this incredibly personal truth, but it was something she couldn't hide from him. Sooner or later he would discover that she wasn't like those sophisticated, experienced women he had dated in the past.

'But how is this possible?' Gabriel was genuinely mystified and shocked to his core. 'You had a boyfriend…'

The mysterious and fictitious boyfriend! How many more times was he going to rear his ugly head? Lucy was sorely tempted to tell him the truth about that, but what would she say? That two years ago she had been so alarmed at Gabriel's aggressive approach that she had fabricated a boyfriend to get rid of him? How flattering was that going to be for a man like Gabriel? A man who enjoyed adulation and was accustomed to the world obeying his commands?

Furthermore, if he became angry enough would he withdraw the terms of his deal? Would her father be back where he had started?

'Er…'

'Don't tell me that the two of you just made do with holding hands and looking longingly into each other's eyes!' He gave a derisive bark of laughter.

'I know a man like you would never understand people who don't put sex at the top of the agenda….'

Gabriel could tell from the embarrassed blush spreading across her cheeks that she was telling the truth—and yet how could that be so? In an age where sex was everywhere, where no holds were barred, how could she have slipped through the net? Especially looking the way she did? Was it her background? He had no idea what her mother was like, or even if she *had* a mother. Had an unstable background with a con man for a father turned her into some kind of buttoned-up prude? And yet she had writhed and squirmed in his arms, had *wanted* to be touched and licked and teased….

'Stop looking at me like that.' Lucy was mortified. 'I'm going to get dressed.' She gathered her overnight back with a jerky movement and scuttled off the bed, still keeping her eyes firmly averted from his incredulous face.

Having just spent the better part of forty-five minutes in the bath, she didn't feel she could justify another forty-five minutes getting into jeans and a T-shirt—and what would be the point anyway? She would still emerge having to face the music....

He was standing by the window when she opened the bathroom door to the bedroom. His first words were, 'I think we should go downstairs...get something to drink...' Even as his mind was playing with the conundrum of a woman of twenty-four who was still a virgin, his eyes were absorbing the terrific sight of her with her hair hanging loose, framing her heart-shaped face in a way that made her look like a living, breathing doll.

Untouched. The thought of being the first man to have her was like a shot of adrenaline, firing his rampant libido. It was a turn-on like nothing in his life before.

'Yes. Of course.' Lucy couldn't look at him. What was he thinking? Maybe that he had purchased sub-standard wares? At great financial cost?

She followed him in subdued silence back down the impressive staircase and into a kitchen that was as expensive as the rest of the house. But she paid little attention to the gleaming speckled black counters and the range of high-tech gadgets and the massive American-style fridge that he was now opening to fetch a jug of fresh orange juice so that he could pour them both a glass.

'Aren't you going to say anything?' she asked eventually. She sat at the kitchen table—a marvel of slate and chrome—and finally stole a look at him from under her lashes.

'What I'd really like is to explore this relationship you had with your boyfriend...because it's not making sense. What kind of guy *was* he?'

'I honestly don't see the point of going into that.' Especially, she thought with a guilty flush, considering he had never even existed. He was now supposed to be in New Zealand. Would she be forced to concoct more information about when he had been living in England? Give him a name? An age? Hobbies?

'It was obviously a relationship that was doomed for disaster if you weren't attracted to one another.'

'I don't want to analyse that...it's over and done with... he's...er...living on the other side of the world now... with...from all accounts...a brand-new wife and a brand-new baby...'

'If you'd accepted my dinner date two years ago I guarantee you wouldn't now be a virgin.'

'You are *so* egotistical!' And yet she knew that he was right. Five seconds in his company was enough to convince her that he had what it took to blow any woman's firmly held principles sky-high. The man should come with a health warning attached.

'Maybe the guy got fed up waiting....' Gabriel didn't know why he was labouring the point. It irked him to imagine that she was perhaps pining for someone who had obviously not cared much for her if he had disappeared across the Atlantic and immediately hitched up with another woman.

'Maybe he did,' Lucy muttered.

'And it still bothers you...?'

She looked up at him, startled. Tempting though it was to expand further on a tale of lost love and broken hearts, she just couldn't do it. 'No,' she told him abruptly. 'What bothers me is not knowing what happens now.'

'What do you *think* happens now?'

'I wouldn't be asking if I knew. I just thought… I just felt it was fair…'

'I get that.' He was looking at her very carefully. Her shy withdrawals and blushing maidenly outrage now seemed to make more sense. He had come on strong and it was no wonder her instinct had been to take flight. 'What if I told you that I can be a very gentle, very tender lover…. I can touch you in a way that will make you open up to me like a flower….'

All those dormant feelings that he had awakened in the bathroom now began stirring back into life at his low, velvety drawl. Her body, once in physical deep freeze, held in storage for the right guy to come along and bring it to life, was making her question the value of preserving herself for someone she hadn't even met yet. Someone she might *never* meet—because who was to say there was a guarantee that there would *be* a Mr Right? She didn't know, and couldn't understand how it was that Mr Wrong could sabotage all her good intentions like this—but he could. Was it his experience? Did he just *know* how to touch a woman so that she stopped being able to think? Was it some special ability of his?

She allowed herself to think about him making love to her and excitement swelled with sudden explosive vigour inside her. The burning memory of his mouth clasped to her nipple sent her body into overdrive.

It would be the very opposite of everything she had ever believed in! Sex without love…in fact, sex without friendship or even passing affection! Did it get any worse? And yet…

She looked at him and his dark, lazy eyes consumed her. Her heart picked up speed.

'But of course I won't.'

'Huh?' Lucy snapped out of her erotic daydream and her mouth fell open in surprise.

'I need something a little stronger than a glass of orange juice.'

Gabriel strolled to the fridge to withdraw a bottle of wine and pour himself a glass. Lucy followed his every small movement with shameful, compulsive fascination. The elegant way he walked, as though he owned the space around him…the flex of muscle beneath his shirt…the strength of his forearms…the powerful width of his shoulders…

She hurriedly looked away as he resumed his seat opposite her. 'Um…you were saying…?' What *had* he been saying? It was impossible to register much when she had been so busy feasting her eyes on him.

'It's off.'

It took a few seconds for his words to sink in. 'What do you mean…? Are you telling me that the deal's off?'

'Regrettably. However tempting I find the notion of sleeping with a virgin…it wouldn't work for me…'

'But we made a deal…we had an arrangement…'

'Deals get broken. It's the way of the world.' Gabriel sipped his wine. His head was still cluttered with images of her underneath him. He would have to do something about that, and quickly.

Lucy sprang to her feet and began pacing the kitchen. She swept her hair back with one hand and finally stood in front of him.

Her body was supple and coltish, and Gabriel cursed himself for not having been able to see that it was also *untouched.* But, hell, how was he to have known?

Should he have explored that weird attraction she had held for him two years ago? How it was that she had lingered in his head long after she had so politely turned him down? And how it was that the notion of having her now, at all costs, had been so irresistible?

Should he somehow have concluded that, for a man as experienced and worldly-wise as he was, the only thing that could have made her stand out was her virginity? No. No sane man would ever have joined the dots and arrived at that conclusion. Virgins over eighteen were as rare as sightings of the dodo bird!

'And what does that mean for my dad?' she asked in a tight voice. 'I told him…' Her lower lip trembled and she bit on it.

'I am a man of honour,' Gabriel said wryly. 'Sit down. You look as though you're about to shatter into a million fragments.' He waited until she was seated, but she was still as tense as a bowstring, with her hands on her thighs and her back ramrod-straight. 'I told you that I would bail your father out and I will. I have already instructed my people to fill in the hole from my own private finances and to close the matter. There will be no record of what your father did. He's in the clear. I also told you that I would pay him off and I still intend to. All things considered, you might say that you've done damn well out of this. Your thieving father lives to steal another day and you don't even have to warm my bed for the favour….'

Lucy's mind had gone a complete blank. The only thing she was aware of was a searing sense of disappointment. It was crazy, but she felt *rejected.*

'You don't look overjoyed. I would expect you to be doing cartwheels round the kitchen at this point.'

'That's very…generous of you…' she said faintly.

'Isn't it?'

'But I don't understand…' She took a deep breath, wiped her clammy hands on her jeans. 'I never realised that being…inexperienced was so awful…'

As conversations went, this was not one for which Gabriel had ever rehearsed. He flushed darkly and wondered how it was that, despite being out of pocket, and with no means of recouping his lost funds, he was reduced to feeling *bad.* Her huge sea-green eyes were staring at him with such honest appeal that he just wanted to scoop her into his arms and show her that being a virgin counted for pretty much everything, that it was a prize for which any red-blooded male would give his eye teeth. Any red-blooded male except him, as it happened.

'This isn't about you,' he told her abruptly.

'If it's not about me, then who on earth is it about?'

'You should be happy. I've just let you off the hook. If you get your things together, I would be more than happy for my driver to return you to the station.'

'My ticket's for tomorrow.' Lucy said the first thing that came to her head. 'And, by the way, I'm very happy. I just wondered… I'm just curious…'

Gabriel vaulted out of his chair, debated whether to have another glass of fortifying wine, decided against it. Instead he helped himself to some water and drank the glass down in one gulp while he kept an eye on her.

'Look…' He sat back down but he felt uncomfortable in his own skin—restless, as though his body couldn't contain the levels of energy leaping through it.

He didn't do soul-searching conversations. There were some men who were good at that sort of thing. He wasn't one of them. But she was still staring at him with those big green eyes and there was no way that he could tell her that a woman just shouldn't ask that sort of question. It wasn't cool. Or maybe there were women who would. How would he know? He had never been in this position before.

'In case you haven't got the message yet, I'm not the kind of guy who's into commitment. I treat my women well…better than well…but I never encourage them to think that there's any more than what I'm prepared to give. You're inexperienced, Lucy. I may be many things, but I'm not into callously hurting girls just because I happen to be attracted to them and just because I can have them. Although…' he allowed himself a self-denigrating smile '…don't think you would be here now if, as you say, I hadn't used unnecessary coercion…'

'No.'

'I firmly believe that all's fair in love and war—but you're a virgin and you're therefore vulnerable. I don't need you getting in over your head.'

'I don't even *like* you. How would I be getting in over my head?'

'If you disliked me that much you would be running for the front door right now with your bags in your hand. I turn you on, and maybe you're a little curious to see where that leads, but there's too much scope for it to lead to places I have no intention of going.'

Lucy was distracted sufficiently to ask, 'You intend to stay a bachelor forever?'

'I prefer to think of it as the foreseeable future.' He shrugged, and a lifetime of cynicism was in that casual gesture. 'This is not something I share with very many people….' *None*. 'My father was married six times. He was the very opposite of a commitment-phobe. He embraced the institution of marriage with whole-hearted enthusiasm. It would have been commendable were it not for the fact that he also embraced infidelity with equal enthusiasm. He once tried to tell me that it was because *he loved women….*'

Gabriel gave a short, derisive, humourless laugh. 'I tend to see it rather differently. It's hard for that argument to carry weight when a man is compelled to marry his latest squeeze, only for that squeeze to be superceded by another model, all in the name of *love*. The marriages became humdrum and routine…my father began getting itchy feet.' He hadn't meant to launch into a prolonged explanation along these lines, but she was listening so damn well, and the past was rushing up at him with such speed…

Well, what was the big deal in telling her this? he asked himself. It wasn't as though she was going to get any ideas…she wasn't going to see one confidence as a sign of greater things to come…

Moreover, he might not have instigated this situation from the purest of motives, but he *could* have just told her to leave without explanation. He could have sent her on her very fortunate, merry way with all those unanswered questions in her head. But had he? No. And wasn't that an indication of his upstanding nature?

'I suppose, on the plus side, I was the only child from all his careless philandering. Maybe somewhere the old man had a conscience after all.'

'You hated him?'

Gabriel looked at her with some surprise. 'Not at all. In his own way he was a very good father. He simply had no self-control. He was clever enough to set up a trust fund for me that he couldn't get into in his weaker moments. It enabled me to be educated abroad. It was a blessing, considering the rest of his earnings invariably went on alimony. He had a good brain, and was a good entrepreneur, but he was always in a situation of *making ends meet* because ex-wives can be costly.'

'And your mother?'

'My mother was one of his victims. Wife number three, as a matter of fact. It broke her heart when he went off her and began seeing wife-to-be number four. She never recovered from him and she died when I was eight, miserable and bitter.'

Lucy gasped and instinctively reached out to him. 'How awful.'

'It was a long time ago.'

'And what happened to you?'

'Oh, I lived with my father until he died, and I was subjected to three more stepmothers and intermittent spells of marital bliss followed by bitter wrangling. I should have hated the old man but I didn't. I learned from him. And here's the moral of what I'm telling you: you're vulnerable. You'll inevitably end up getting hurt. I won't be the one responsible. I learnt pretty young that if you want sex it's better to have it without any unrealistic expectations on either side.'

Lucy had the feeling that she was staring at someone who came from a different planet from hers. Her parents could not be more in love with one another. She cherished the dream of that happy-ever-after relationship while he derided it.

'Go and get your bag, Lucy.'

'My parents are expecting me to be in London for the weekend,' Lucy mumbled.

Plus, they were under the impression that she was *dating* Gabriel. They hadn't asked her whether she would be *sleeping* with him—they would trust her to be holding true to the principles they had instilled in her. Her friends also thought that she was on a date, of sorts. She couldn't face getting the evening train back… There would be humiliating questions that she would have to answer. She would be forced to say that they had broken up after only one date because…what…? He didn't like her? He found her company boring? Backward? Too rough around the edges?

At least if she stuck this weekend out she could maybe

do a couple more—visit London and stay somewhere cheap—at the end of which she would vaguely suggest that they hadn't hit it off after all.

But to return home after only a few hours…

'Well, I'm pretty sure they won't be disappointed to have you back home without having had to endure the unsavoury business of sleeping with their benefactor.'

'I…I think, actually, I might go and have a look around London. After all the effort to get here it seems a shame to waste my trip.'

'I would have thought it was anything *but* a wasted trip.'

'You know, I'd really like to explain about my fath—'

'Drop it. That's all history. I wasn't interested in hearing excuses then and I'm even less interested now.'

'It doesn't feel right to accept money from you—'

'Are you telling me that you would rather I held you captive here with no "release date", as you put it?'

'No, of course not!'

Gabriel was right. She had been given her ticket out, so why wasn't she running? Did it *matter* that her friends might ask a few questions about her early return? That her mother might wonder aloud why her so-called date had gone wrong? Her father had been bailed out and she had her precious virginity intact.

So why wasn't she shrieking with joy? Why was she harking back to those weird, wonderful things she had felt when he had touched her? Could it be that she had psyched herself up to sleeping with him and she was now in the grip of a puzzling anticlimax? Had she spent so much time being angry with him for making her pay a price that was so high for the favour he was bestowing on her that she had failed to recognise the very simple truth—which was that she was actually *turned on* by him? Against all odds? He was sexy beyond belief, and she was only human, after all.

Not to mention the fact that her lack of experience hadn't equipped her with the necessary weapons to withstand the onslaught of his blazing personality…

Now he was writing her off as an ill-judged mistake. He was a predator who had sized up his prey and homed in for the kill only to realise that the prey in question wasn't what he had had in mind after all. He was letting her go. She still had no idea what it was about her that had provoked him into giving her a second glance, but she did know that for Gabriel Diaz the sea was replete with fish. Lose one and there would be plenty others.

'Perhaps we could…do something…?' she suggested timidly. 'I mean…I don't suppose you made any plans for today…'

'You want to *do something*?' Gabriel raised his eyebrows disbelievingly. She was priceless. He had just dismissed her, having kindly pointed out her glaring limitations when it came to the role of mistress, and yet here she was, hesitantly asking if they could *do something*! 'Do what?'

'I've never really been to any of the sights in London…'

'Hang on a minute. I'm the arrogant bastard who blackmailed you into a position you supposedly hated, and yet now that you've been released from that position, you want to *hang around*? *Go sightseeing?* You have no idea what you're dealing with…'

'What *am* I dealing with?'

She couldn't control a wicked shiver of anticipation. She had been raised with all her moral values in place, raised on Sunday school and thank-you notes and Girl Guides. She had been raised to fall in love with one of life's good guys, get married, have babies and live in a cottage in the country. Gabriel Diaz was *not* a good guy. His values were all in the wrong places. He was unapologetically dangerous and he was warning her off him. She wasn't just playing with fire…she was walking into an open flame.

'I… It's okay… I'll get my stuff…'

She stood up, but he caught her wrist before she could turn away. 'I'll take you sightseeing.' Gabriel could feel the rapid beating of her pulse. This was not what he should be doing, but that hesitancy in her eyes, at war with the delicacy of her body and the innocence of her come-on, excited him. 'But make no mistake. If you find yourself out of your depth the time for rescue rafts will be over.'

'I've always wanted to go to Madame Tussauds….'

At a little after six the perfect weather finally broke. They had had their fill of Madame Tussauds, but Lucy had barely taken anything in. All the time they had traipsed through the crowds she had been hyper-sensitive to the man next to her. She wondered what she was doing. She wasn't a *dangerous* kind of girl. The first time she had met him she had been confused and intimidated by the directness of his approach and had ducked for cover. So what was going on now?

She just knew that whenever she looked at him and saw the brooding intensity in his dark, fathomless eyes she couldn't contain the thrill of excitement that threaded its way through her veins like a toxic drug.

Apparently he had never taken a woman sightseeing before. But while she'd nervously chattered her way through the exhibitions, he'd drily provided historical detail to some of the wax figures. He seemed to know a vast amount of information. However successful he was when it came to making money, he was also obviously amazingly well read.

She'd asked him why he didn't enjoy just walking around London. He'd told her that it wasn't his thing. Every time they'd touched on anything remotely personal he'd made sure to send her a guarded warning that she should be careful.

Lucy's brain refused to register any of those warnings. She heard his voice and something in her melted. It was almost as if, under threat, she had responded with anger at his arrogance in bargaining with her body, but with the threat removed something strange, weirdly exciting and entirely unexpected had been allowed to rise to the surface.

After Madame Tussauds they'd had a very late lunch at a very expensive restaurant close to his house. She imagined that it was the sort of place he always took his women. Her jeans had not been remarked upon, but she knew that his wealth would allow him to go anywhere with anyone without question. He was someone to whom normal rules did not apply and he accepted that as his due.

They were leaving the restaurant when the heavens opened and the rain bucketed down with such unexpected force that there was no time to find shelter.

'How far are we from your house?' Lucy had to shout over the clatter of the raindrops slamming against the pavement and the buildings.

'Too far.' He held up one hand to hail a taxi and she impulsively reached across to stop him.

'It's warm. It's summer rain. We could make a dash for it....'

'Not going to happen.'

'Why? Is getting wet something you don't do either?'

Gabriel stared down into her green eyes. He hadn't always been wealthy beyond most people's wildest dreams. He hadn't always been able to snap his fingers and see the world drop at his feet. He'd had an uncomfortable childhood, watching his mother get too fond of the bottle and then, later, before he was packed off to boarding school at the age of thirteen, hiding out in his bedroom, where the sounds of his father's latest disintegrating marriage couldn't be heard through headphones and loud music.

He had witnessed firsthand the effects of a marital break-up. The constant house-moves because ex-wives needed accommodating. Possessions that were there one minute and gone the next. He had determined that he would live his life differently. For starters, no addiction to walking down the aisle with anyone. For another thing, no fluctuating finances. Total control would be his driving force. He had become inured to the things he had striven to avoid, thanks to his considerable wealth, but now Lucy was staring up at him with just a hint of laughter in her eyes.

'You could always get your clothes dry-cleaned. Or you could get one of your lackeys to take them to the dry cleaner for you, if you don't do trips to dry cleaners...'

The rain continued to pour down on them. Gabriel conceded defeat. He nodded in the direction of his house. He had no intention of running, and he wished to God he had had the foresight to carry an umbrella with him, but still he got a kick watching her as she ran ahead of him, happily getting soaked to the skin.

She was waiting in front of the house when he got there, hopping from one foot to the other. Her hair hung around her in wet blond strands, clinging to her neck and back and arms. There was a flash of lightning and a crack of sharp, sudden thunder and he unlocked the front door and pushed it open to let her precede him.

She smelled of the rain. Even in London it was a clean, fresh smell that filled his nostrils like powerful incense.

Lucy felt goosebumps on her arms as he shut the heavy door behind them, sealing off the noisy clamour of the rain, which now became a muted background sound. It was cooler inside than it had been outside. She turned to him to find his dark eyes fastened on her—but he broke the spell by walking away, telling her over his shoulder that she would have to get changed.

Lucy felt wild and giddy, and her head was full to bursting with thoughts of Gabriel. He had no morals and was bitter beyond his years…he had an unshakeable belief that the only thing that mattered was money, that it was the currency for buying anything and anyone he wanted… He had tried to buy *her* and used the threat of prison for her father as leverage, and he had done it without a shadow of guilt or discomfort…. He was arrogant, and unapologetic about it….

On the other hand there was an integrity in his not assuming a right to her body when he had discovered that she had never slept with a man before…and there was decency in the fact that he had not reneged on his promise to bail her father out even though he had failed to get the exchange he had anticipated. Although his moral codes left a lot to be desired, and his aims in life were far removed from hers, weren't there extenuating circumstances? Hadn't his background made him the man he was? He was emotionally cold, and would never engage fully with a woman…but there had been humour when he had filled in the gaps in her knowledge of history, a spellbinding intelligence, and weren't those engaging qualities in themselves?

As long-term partners went, winning the lottery was a surer bet—but who wanted a long-term partner…?

And when had anyone ever made her feel like this in her life before?

She knew that was the million-dollar question that had been nagging away at the back of her mind. When she stopped telling herself how ridiculous it was to be attracted to a man like him there was a space in her head that was immediately filled with the memory of him holding her in the bathroom, kissing her, running his hands underneath her T-shirt while her body throbbed and vibrated like an engine revving to go.

'Why are you still standing out here?'

Lucy started and swivelled round to look at him. He was holding a mug of something hot and had removed his wet clothes. He was now in an old T-shirt and a pair of low-slung chinos and barefoot. There must be a laundry room nestled somewhere behind the kitchen, she thought, her heart beating fast.

'I…I was just about to go and get changed. I don't want to drip all over your expensive flooring…the rugs…I don't want to ruin them…'

'I think the expensive flooring and the soft furnishings will survive the experience,' Gabriel said drily.

She was looking at him the way a starving man might look at a banquet. Women looked at him. He was used to that. But he wasn't used to women looking at him as though they would give anything in the world *not* to. Lucy's gauche responses set alarm bells ringing in his head, but for once he was finding himself powerless to exercise the self-control on which he prided himself. Instead he was staring back at her—a long, lazy, assessing stare, his eyes roving with bold appreciation over the way her wet clothes were clinging to her body. He could see the definition of her bra underneath the T-shirt and he was overcome with craving—primitive, uncontrollable craving.

'You can look at me all you want,' Gabriel drawled, moving to lean idly against the doorframe, 'but the second you touch all bets are off….'

'What do you mean?'

'You've had your freedom card. There are no more where that came from. I can only do Mr Nice Guy for a limited period of time, and the window on that is now closed. So stare all you want, but if you want more then you're going to have to play by my rules—and my rules don't apply to anyone who's looking for a safe harbour....'

He turned on his heel and headed back to the kitchen, and Lucy was left to consider what he had said—and to try and work out where the girl who had left her village and her safe life had disappeared to.

CHAPTER FIVE

'SO, AM I going to get my driver to take you to the station? Ditch your ticket. It's easy enough for me to buy you a new one....'

Lucy had finally managed to locate Gabriel. He had migrated from the kitchen and his hot drink to the sitting room and a glass of deep red wine. She'd had to search a number of rooms before she found him, and now knew every room was decorated to the same high standard. It was an enormous house. She had no idea how many bathrooms and bedrooms were scattered over the top three floors, but on the ground floor alone there appeared to be a number of sitting areas, a vast conservatory overlooking a garden, and a study—and all this in addition to the kitchen and whatever else lay beyond it. Certainly the laundry room from which he had earlier extracted his change of clothing.

He was sprawled on a leather sofa, nursing his drink, with his laptop flipped open on the low glass coffee table in front of him. He looked cool, composed, effortlessly elegant.

Lucy, who had planned on coming to London with the least flattering clothes she possessed—because why on earth should she make an effort when she was obeying orders under duress?—felt instantly inadequate. He had mentioned disliking her combat trousers, so those had been priority items when she had packed. Her T-shirts were loose and faded, and her trainers, she had fondly imagined, would be handy should she feel the need to run very fast in the opposite direction.

She hadn't banked on getting here and finding all her preconceived notions turned on their head.

'Well?' Gabriel sipped his wine and looked at her over the rim of his glass. He had no intention of helping her out on this score. He wasn't going to ease her into his bed, he wasn't going to tempt her, and he certainly wasn't going to give her any excuse for turning on him and accusing him, for a second time, of assaulting her. That gross exaggeration still stuck in his throat. But with unerring instinct he knew that to someone like Lucy freedom of choice would be the most difficult path. He also knew that it would get him what he wanted—and he wanted *her*.

With all his conditional clauses in place, and his provisos, warnings and barriers in full working order, he looked forward to the sweetest of conquests.

So he didn't rush her into a decision. He just kept his eyes on her, noting her fluctuations of colour and her awkward, hovering stance by the door.

'Perhaps I could stay the night.' Lucy wondered whether she had committed to sleeping with him by saying that and felt inclined to backtrack, but she held her ground.

This was all so crazy, but once she had taken it on board—once she had given house room to the reality that she was violently, helplessly attracted to him—she had squashed all her girlish ideals and succumbed to the most wonderful feeling of liberation.

'In that case let me get you a drink.'

'I don't usually…'

'I'm getting the picture that there are a lot of things that you *don't usually…*' There was a concealed drinks cabinet in the sitting room and he poured her some wine and then sat back down. 'And you can stop standing by the door like a scared rabbit….'

'What did you see in me?'

'Come again?'

'What did you see in me? I mean…two years ago…and now…what did you see in me?'

'You have a habit of asking the most unnerving questions,' Gabriel murmured, watching as she primly sat on one of the chairs facing him and wondering when she would get up the courage to actually enter his radius. She was so unlike the confident, pushy women he associated with—women who would have removed his drink from his hand a long time ago and walked him up the stairs, making it perfectly clear where they wanted the evening to end.

'I'm just curious. I know you don't like the stuff I wear…'

'What man would? I like to see my women in dresses.' He pictured that slender, eye-catching, lightly tanned body in something small and revealing and decided that the thought didn't appeal. 'Floaty affairs. Long.'

'Really? Because those pictures on the internet of you with your dates…well, they were all incredibly…er…underdressed…'

'How long did you spend gazing at me on your computer?'

'Not long!'

Gabriel shrugged, but he was smiling. 'I was attracted to your lack of artifice. I spotted that as soon as I laid eyes on you on that bike. No make-up, wind in your hair, glowing. I liked that trait then and I like it now. I don't meet many women who are natural and straightforward…'

He had a way of looking at her that was as erotic as a physical caress.

'I mean,' he expanded, 'you ask questions other women would shy away from. And you blush. That rates as a virtually extinct art form.'

'So you're attracted to me because I'm a novelty…?'

Gabriel frowned. 'Where are you going with this line of questioning?'

'It's important for me to know how the ground lies.'

'Does it matter why I'm attracted to you? I just am. In fact, I'd much rather you were sitting here next to me instead of over there, but I'm not about to push you into anything. Believe me, if I thought you could handle me then we wouldn't be having this conversation, and we wouldn't be sitting on two chairs like a couple of strangers making small talk.'

'But we *are* a couple of strangers…'

'That's a situation I would have remedied the second you got off the train.'

Gabriel's way of thinking was clearly alien to Lucy. He had no interest in getting to know her. He would chat to her, but his primary interest was making love. Everything else around that main event would be of little concern to him. He was drawn to her because she was different from what he was used to. How different he had only just discovered. Had he known at the time, he wouldn't have made the mistake of pursuing her. No make-up and wind in her hair was very different from *virginal.*

'Someone doesn't stop being a stranger because you sleep with them….'

'Possibly not, but it's a start….'

He sent her a slow, wolfish grin that made her tummy flip over and turned her even breathing into a sharp, breathless pant.

'And when do you start getting bored?'

Lucy felt as though she was tiptoeing round him, trying to find a way into that complex mind that thought so differently from hers. He had explained his reasons for avoiding commitment, but he had spoken so dispassionately that he might have been talking about someone else and not himself. She wondered whether she would really and truly be able to take on a man as impenetrable as Gabriel, but even as she was asking herself the question her responsive body was supplying the answer.

'You sound like an interviewer. I know you're in new terrain here, but loosen up. I can't tell you when I start getting bored with a woman! How would any man be able to answer a question like that? All I can do is repeat what I've told you before. I have ground rules, and I suppose when a woman—any woman—starts thinking that she can stray over the boundaries I usually see fit to call it a day.'

Looking at him, Lucy felt that it was important for her to hear all this. Sleeping around was nothing for Gabriel, and he sought out women who shared his approach. But for Lucy sleeping with Gabriel would be a big deal. She would be acting completely out of character, allowing a physical side to her she had never suspected existed to take precedence over logic and reason. If he had his ground and his boundary lines then it was important for her to recognise that—just as it was important for her to let him know her feelings on the matter.

She couldn't believe that she was thinking like this. She had always assumed that she would only ever be attracted to a man for whom she had strong feelings; and it was unsettling to accept that attraction could have laws of its own that had little or nothing to do with feelings and emotions. It was just pure luck that it was a discovery that she hadn't made earlier.

'And too many women do,' Gabriel admitted heavily. 'Despite the fact that I'm perfectly honest at the onset of any relationship. Sooner or later there's a tendency for them to become clingy and demanding.'

'How awful for you.'

Gabriel looked at her narrowly. 'Am I detecting some sarcasm there?'

'Not at all. It must be difficult when you're so clear about what you *don't* want a woman to be….'

Gabriel threw her a slashing smile that reminded her why she was in this position now, helplessly treading water in the face of his potent masculine charisma.

'Amongst other things, this is part of your appeal,' he continued huskily, watching her carefully with those clever dark eyes.

'What do you mean?'

'You don't have any pointless girlish fantasies about me. You've seen me for what I am since the very second I made you that offer you couldn't refuse. There's no chance that you're going to go romantic on me. There's no chance that you're going to suddenly decide that you want to hear the sound of wedding bells. You're not going to be tempted into thinking that you can change me. Call me selfish, but I like all of that.'

Lucy barely recognised herself in his description. She had *always* had dreams of wedding bells, and she was a fully signed-up member of the romantic club, but she could see where he was going. He had approached her in a manner that left no illusions, and she had made it clear to him that she didn't like him—so if they ended up in bed together it would literally be a case of sexual attraction minus anything else. It would be the ultimate no-strings-attached affair.

She was shocked at the heady sense of power that simple

recognition invested her with. In a very brief space of time his powerful sex appeal and the open invitation in his lazy, assessing eyes had combined to chip away at her resolve.

'You're right. I don't like you….' Although with some confusion she recalled that there had been times during their day spent sightseeing when he had made her laugh and she had completely forgotten the angst that had been her companion on the train to London. She sidelined that thought with a little frown.

'It's so refreshing the way you speak your mind,' Gabriel drawled. 'I've never been in the company of a woman who doesn't think twice about being offensive.'

Sitting on the sofa while she occupied the chair opposite was getting to him. Especially when he knew where they would be ending up. It was like being invited to sit at a table groaning with food and knowing that you couldn't touch a thing…*yet.* The anticipation was killing him. He was a man who took what he wanted and had never been made to wait. Patience was not his middle name, and that had served him well in all his dealings to strike while the iron was hot.

'I don't see myself as an offensive person,' Lucy said slowly.

Gabriel drummed his fingers restlessly on his thigh and toyed with the idea of putting an end to the chat by hauling her over his shoulder and carrying her upstairs to his bedroom.

'Why don't you like me?' he heard himself ask, and winced at the crassness of the question—because other people's opinions of him were irrelevant as far as he was concerned. Instead of prolonging the conversation he should be moving up a gear and heading the chat in the right direction.

'Why do you think?'

'My approach may have been a little unorthodox, but that aside...'

Lucy looked at his perfectly serious face and wanted to burst out laughing. She had noticed during the course of the day that he had a unique way of dealing with people and with situations. He didn't analyse them and nor did he see any failings in his direct approach to getting what he wanted. He had told her in passing that he had once gone to see a movie—which seemed to be a rare event for him—and, not wanting to share the theatre with anyone else, had simply solved the problem by buying all the seats and ensuring complete privacy for himself and whatever woman he had on his arm at the time.

When she had told him that normal people didn't do stuff like that, he had shrugged and said, 'Why not? Makes sense as far as I'm concerned.'

'You're too cold,' Lucy explained, thinking hard, her brow pleated into a small frown. 'Too removed, too insensitive to other people...'

'Enough! I disagree with you on all fronts, but I'm not about to have an argument. Was your ex-boyfriend warm and engaging? A good cook? He couldn't have been that exciting if you never managed to make it past the bedroom door.'

Colour flooded Lucy's cheeks but she held her ground. The ex-boyfriend might not have existed, but *no one* had made it past her bedroom door. 'That's why I don't understand how...why I'm still here,' she confessed honestly. 'I mean...'

Gabriel held up one hand, because he had a feeling where this was going. 'I think I'm about to be treated to another rambling description of everything you dislike about me and I'm tired of talking.' He sat back and stretched his arm along the back of the sofa.

'What do you want to do?'

'I think we both know what I want to do—just like we both know what *you* want to do. So instead of spending the next three hours trying to work out the *whys* let's just cut to the chase.'

He didn't make a move towards her. He just kept her pinned to the spot until she forged a trembling path towards him.

'Don't forget,' Gabriel murmured softly, 'you leave your overactive conscience behind the second you enter my bedroom....'

Lucy nodded.

'And relax.' He smiled crookedly. 'Trust me.'

He reached out and ran one lean finger along her clenched fist. A series of mini-explosions detonated in her. Arousal as fierce as it was sudden slammed into her with the terrifying force of a runaway train.

She followed him in a trance up the stairs to his bedroom—the very same bedroom that she had earlier regarded with such trepidation, when she had thought that she might be sharing that king-sized bed with him, a prisoner of circumstance.

'You're doing that scared rabbit thing again....' Gabriel edged her away from the bedroom door and led her very gently towards a big window that overlooked his back garden. 'What do you think?' He could feel the slight but unmistakable tremor running through her slender body like quicksilver and he raised his hand to massage the back of her neck gently, underneath the thick sweep of her hair.

Lucy stared down at a small but impressive garden, beautifully landscaped and not overlooked. The warmth of his hand on her neck was just right, putting her at ease. 'I prefer the garden to the house.'

'I have no idea what plants are out there. I handed the

whole job over to professionals when I moved here five years ago.'

'That's very lazy.'

'Maybe if I'd known you at the time you could have come and sorted it all out for me. I would have enjoyed watching you in a little pair of shorts and a T-shirt out there....'

He turned her to face him and her heart skipped a beat as she looked up into his dark, beautiful face.

'I wouldn't have enjoyed being watched.' She had never been drawn to dressing up to attract the attention of men. She had always left that to her more flamboyant friends. She enjoyed hearing about their escapades but it wasn't for her. She wondered if that was a legacy of having much older, quieter parents.

Gabriel wondered whether that accounted for the boyfriend running to New Zealand to bond with sheep. He relished the challenge of teaching her to enjoy *him* watching her.

He circled her waist under the T-shirt, and as his hands drifted higher he could feel the rapid beat of her heart under her ribcage. There was nothing voluptuous or overt about her, and her slim body was a joy to touch. The thought of some of his thrusting, busty girlfriends, with their smouldering mascara-heavy eyes and their lacy leave-nothing-to-the-imagination underwear, was vaguely distasteful.

He kept his eyes fixed on her spectacularly pretty, fresh face as his fingers came into contact with her bra. He skimmed two fingers under the top of each cup, tracing a delicate line down to her nipples, and his groin was aching as her eyes fluttered and she breathed in sharply.

Without moving away, he slowly unclasped the bra. Lucy moaned softly and allowed him to strip her gently of the T-shirt and then of her bra. She closed her eyes when she was half undressed, her breasts bared for his inspection.

'You have beautiful breasts,' Gabriel rasped huskily.

'They're too small.'

'They're perfect.' He cupped them and massaged them gently. He wasn't going to rush. 'It would be nice if you opened your eyes.'

Lucy peeped at him. This wasn't the arrogant, super-rich, super-confident guy who had so alarmed her two years ago, and nor was he the manipulative tyrant who had so angered her when he had thrown down his gauntlet and forced her into a deal she resented. This was someone smiling and putting her at ease, keeping his eyes pinned to hers while he continued to caress her breasts until she began finding it difficult to catch her breath.

He edged her towards his bed and then stood back so that he could remove his shirt. Lucy teetered back a few steps, bumped into the base of the bed and fell onto the soft, silky duvet. She looked compulsively at the broad, hard expanse of his chest—not smooth and hairless, like the boys she had known, but roughened with dark hair. A man's chest. She propped herself up on her elbows. So what if she was staring? She couldn't help herself. He was magnificent. How could she restrain herself from greedily devouring the sight?

He hooked his fingers over the waistband of his chinos and tugged them slightly down, so that she could see the defined muscles of his pelvis, the narrowness of his waist. He must work out like a demon, she thought in a daze, and if he didn't then he had been unfairly blessed.

She looked as if she'd forgotten that she was half clothed, her breasts pointed up at him. Her rosebud nipples were a massive turn-on, and Gabriel hesitated to strip completely naked. He was not in the slightest self-conscious of his body, but would his erection spook her?

'I enjoy you watching me like this,' he murmured, moving towards her on the bed.

Lucy smiled. His eyes glittered with dark, rampant appreciation and she felt a sudden sense of heady power. It was nothing like she had ever felt in her life before. She *wanted* to throw off the rest of her clothes and let him touch her all over. She remembered how she had burned for him in the bathroom, before she had backed away, and she wanted that burning again.

Had she really been saving herself for the right guy? Or had she just never been turned on enough actually to make it to bed with anyone? That was the question playing at the back of her mind as he loomed over her before bending down to unzip her trousers.

'I hate these trousers….'

'I know.' Lucy shot him a sheepish smile and lowered her eyes. 'That's why I brought them with me.'

'Did you think that if you dressed badly enough I might be put off wanting to haul you into my arms and carry you off to my bed like a caveman?'

'Something like that.'

'It wouldn't have worked. Unfortunately there's nothing you could ever wear that would have that effect on me. But I'd still like to see you in a dress….'

The trousers were now off, and Gabriel's mouth twitched in amusement at her functional cotton underwear—the sort of underwear that was sold in packets of six from a department store and definitely not the kind that any woman he had dated would have been caught dead wearing.

She was so damned fresh and innocent that he felt a moment of passionate wanting to lock her away in a tower, where no one could lay eyes on her but him. That sudden rush of unexpected possessiveness took him by surprise and he quickly shoved it away, ruthlessly stamping on feelings he neither wanted nor needed.

Lucy lay back. She had released her very long hair and it fanned out around her in a blaze of golden blond, startling against the backdrop of the dark silk duvet cover.

She knew she should be feeling shy, rushing to cover her body, but she wasn't. The opposite. She felt wonderfully brazen. It was something to do with the way he was looking at her—as if she was a delicate morsel he wanted to devour. It was the most amazing experience, and she smiled drowsily at him.

She had no idea how beautiful she was, Gabriel thought. His keen eyes noted the dusting of freckles on her collarbone, the tiny mole by her left breast, the perfect delineation of her nipples. Her stomach was flat and smooth and he could see her hip bones. Once again he wondered what he had ever found appealing in heavy, big breasts and sultry, rounded curves. Lucy's body was slender, but strong from all the outdoor work she did. She led a healthy lifestyle and it showed in her toned, graceful physique.

He gently began pulling down the unappealing underwear and his breathing became unusually laboured as he took in the dark blond, downy curls slanting between her thighs.

'Look at me when I touch you,' he commanded gruffly, then gave her a crooked smile that could have melted a block of ice. 'I want to find out what you like….'

Lucy imagined that she might like everything he did to her. She was loving the way he was simply looking at her now. She desperately wanted him to be as naked as she was, and yet something deep inside her was telling her that he had deliberately left his trousers on so that he could continue to put her at her ease.

She sighed as he moved over her, propping himself up on his hands so that he could stare down at her flushed face. When she raised her arms to wind them around his neck he gently but firmly laid them back at her sides, before bending so that he could lavish his attention on her breasts.

He had died and gone to heaven. Every twitch of her body was an indication of her arousal. It took fierce concentration to keep to what he was doing when he wanted to thrust into her and satisfy the growing ache in his groin.

He clasped her hands in his and licked the stiffened buds of her nipples, teasing them alternately with his tongue. He was getting more and more turned on by her cries and moans and the way she writhed under him, begging for more, and then gasping that she couldn't stand it any longer.

Her nipples were shiny and wet from his mouth and his tongue. Her eyes flickered open as he drew back, and then widened when he reached behind him and gently cupped the feminine mound between her legs before easing his fingers into the slippery moistness that was eagerly awaiting his touch.

'Do you like this?' He found the aroused bud and teased it with his finger, watched the rosy blush that invaded her cheeks.

'Gabriel…' she moaned.

'Have you been touched like this before?' Crazy question, but he really wanted to know—and when she shook her head he couldn't contain the soaring triumph that ripped through him. On and on he continued to rub that small throbbing peak. He knew just when to ease the maddening caress of his fingers and when to pick up the tempo so that her body began to spasm.

She could have wept with frustration when he stopped

so that he could kiss her stomach, move down to her belly button and then…down to that most intimate of places. She was well beyond any inhibition. She let him ease her legs apart and arched back to accommodate his darting, exploring tongue, which was finding the place that turned her on and lathering attention on it.

She curled her fingers into his hair and loosened her legs wider. She had never thought her body was capable of being so exquisitely tortured. His tongue against her was sending her spiralling higher and higher, and yet still he wouldn't let her reach the final climax. She was completely at his mercy, wanting him to take her wholly. She wanted him to fill her and she was shocked at her own driving need.

She was not at all intimidated when he eventually pulled back and removed the rest of his clothes. She wanted to touch his impressive arousal. She watched as he donned protection, but she hardly had time to scramble onto her elbows before he had resumed his position over her. He nudged at her gently, edging himself into her dampness, telling her not to tense and smoothing over her natural inclination to stiffen up.

He was unbelievably tender, moving slowly, letting her relax. Only when he began pushing harder into her did she cry out, but the instant was lost as sensations began driving through her—wonderful sensations as his manhood pressed into her. He thrust deeper and harder and she melted, abandoning herself to wave upon wave of pleasure until she was exhausted.

Gabriel was on a high such as he had never known before. He had had lovers who were experienced in the art of doing anything in any position, and yet he couldn't recall ever having this feeling of soaring satisfaction as he climaxed.

'Bloody hell,' he growled, subsiding against her on the bed. 'That was…incredible…'

Lucy sighed and curled against him. She still couldn't quite believe that she had jumped from one extreme to the other in the blink of an eye. The girl who had so resentfully left Somerset was not the girl on this bed now. How had that happened? How could sexual attraction be so persuasive and so instant? How could it drive you in one direction even though your mind was telling you to run fast in the other?

She rested her hand on his chest and he covered her hand with his, turned onto his side so that he was facing her.

'So…' Gabriel couldn't get enough of her smooth, soft, supple body. Her nipple was peeping out at him beneath the crook of her arm and he knew he could have made love to her all over again. But it seemed inappropriate, given the circumstances. Was she sore? Tender down there? His hand itched to tease her slowly back into a state of readiness for him.

'So…?'

'You took a circuitous route to get where I wanted you to be from the start….'

Lucy blushed. 'I…I'm not sure how all this has happened…' she confessed. 'When I got on that train I thought that if we ended up in bed it would be…'

'A nightmare?'

'Something like that.'

'You underestimate the power of sex.'

Lucy opened her mouth to protest but decided that she didn't have a leg to stand on.

'So what happens now?' she asked with a little frown. 'I mean…now that we've slept together…does that mean…?'

'That the debt's been paid?'

Lucy nodded. She felt a sense of clammy dismay that he might now get rid of her, having had his fill. She suspected that at the back of his mind the challenge of having a woman who had once turned him down had been irresistible. With that challenge no longer there, would he still be driven to sleep with her? It would pay her to remind herself that he could have anyone—why would he choose *her* when her novelty value had already been lost?

Her body was already missing the feel of his in anticipation of being told that she had fulfilled her part of the contract.

'Your father *did* embezzle from my company…and he most certainly *would* have served jail time—so, no… You might have a little way to go with that deal we made…'

He ran his hand along her waist and then over her thigh, where his lazy, circular, feathery light touch had the intended effect of making her body liquefy.

'Sorry to disappoint you…but you're *not* disappointed, are you? You had your chance to bolt and you turned it down…' It was a richly satisfying thought.

'You're very egotistical,' Lucy said truthfully.

'I just enjoy getting what I want—and what I still want for the foreseeable future is…*you*…' He slipped two fingers into the dampness between her thighs and kept his eyes firmly glued to hers. 'It's gratifying to know that the feeling's mutual….'

Lucy knew that she should feel degraded and angry—but she didn't. In fact, the only thing she felt was turned on. She closed her eyes and parted her mouth as he began to stroke the tight raised bud of her clitoris.

She was so wonderfully responsive! Gabriel couldn't conceive that she might consider one night full and final payment!

She climaxed with soft moans and was embarrassed

when she opened her eyes to find him looking at her with a half-smile.

'Sorry,' she mumbled. 'That wasn't satisfying for you.'

'You'd be surprised… I'm a generous kind of guy. I like giving pleasure. But right now I think it might be a good idea for us to get showered, and then we can do a little more sightseeing before we have dinner somewhere.'

'I haven't brought any clothes to wear out.'

'In which case, we can do our sightseeing at Selfridges. Lots of clothes there. I don't do shopping with women, but I feel I could get a kick out of buying clothes for you.'

'I'm sorry, I can't accept that.'

'Come again?'

'I don't want you buying anything for me.' Was that because she wanted to kid herself that she hadn't been bought? Lucy thought with consternation. Did she want to read more into this than there really was because that way she could make sense of her inability to control her rebellious body?

'There's not a woman on this planet who doesn't like having things bought for them.' He traced the outline of one pert nipple and watched as it tightened and reacted to his touch. 'You'll find me a generous lover in more ways than one. For as long as we're together, whatever you want will be yours.'

At that moment Lucy imagined that he could have talked her into anything. He had taken her body to places of unimaginable delight. He had made her aware of lust as something wildly beyond control. But somehow the thought of having clothes and jewellery and *whatever she wanted* bought for her made her feel sick.

'No, Gabriel.'

Gabriel looked at her, startled.

'When this is all…finished…I don't want to think that I owe you anything.'

'That's not what it would be about—'

'It would be—for me. The only time I would ever accept gifts from a guy is from a guy I love.'

Her mouth was a stubborn line and he shook his head with incomprehension and impatience. From the very start he had seen the advantages of bedding a woman he fancied without any of the complications that usually arose. He had envisaged a relationship based on sex alone, and here she was offering him just the no-strings-attached liaison he wanted. So why was he feeling annoyed?

He reminded himself that she was his, that she had come to him of her own free will, and he relaxed.

'We'll see…' he murmured. 'Now, let's go have a shower—or else I'm going to have to do a bit more than pleasure you with my fingers, and right now I don't think you're up to taking me…are you?'

'Maybe not *right* now.'

'Shame. But by tonight I think we'll both be ready.'

'Yes.' She blushed fiery pink, but why pretend otherwise? She might be a little tender now, but already she couldn't wait for them to be back in this bedroom—for him to be making love to her again…and again…and again…

CHAPTER SIX

LUCY WASN'T ENTIRELY sure when lust started becoming something much more dangerously significant.

She had entered Gabriel's exotic and rarefied world a little over four months ago. After that first weekend they had established a pattern of weekend visits. On her insistence, she was always the one who made the trip up to London to see him.

Several times he had asked her to stay over on the Sunday night, and it had taken real effort on her part not to cave in. But she knew, with gut instinct that caving in was something *all* his women would have done. It was what he would expect of them. She had stood firm, however, because she had her job to consider, and she wasn't about to start fooling around with that just because Gabriel Diaz crooked his finger and worked his magic.

Twice he had unexpectedly phoned her at work and told her that he had to see her—that he would drive down, that he couldn't focus when all he could think about was getting rid of her clothes and taking her....

She had stood firm on that as well, even though just hearing the urgency in his deep, dark voice had filled her body with a wild, throbbing need.

'I hope you're not doing this because you think that playing hard to get will hold my interest,' he had drawled just a couple of weeks ago, when yet again she had antagonised him by telling him that she didn't want him visiting her.

Lucy had vigorously denied any such thing. Did he really think she was that silly? There were so many ways he had of reminding her that he wasn't in it for the long haul. He wasn't even aware of how glaringly clear he was on the subject.

On more than one occasion he had told her that he never, ever forgot to use protection because the last thing he would want was to find himself trapped in the unwanted role of father. He had firmly closed the door on all discussion to do with her family. He wasn't interested in any personal baggage she might be carrying—especially if it involved something as distasteful as a crooked father. That was a side to her of which he wanted no reminders. For him, she existed exclusively in the realms of sex and desire. Anything else was a distraction and an annoyance.

And yet over time they'd laughed, they'd talked, they'd shared opinions. She teased him about his inability to do anything in the kitchen and he kept trying to buy her clothes—which she refused. She now had a couple more dresses to call her own, and even a pair of boots that were not, strictly speaking, functional. They protected her feet from the cold—and it was certainly getting cold now, as winter began to replace what had been a mild autumn—but with heels at over three inches high walking was often a challenge.

Should she have been more aware of the signs that what she was feeling went beyond sex? When should it have occurred to her that she was living from Monday to Friday afternoon in a state of barely suppressed excitement at the prospect of seeing him? That this was not healthy? When should she have stopped pretending that good sex was something non-addictive and that it never led anywhere? How could she have been so stupid as not to realise that making love and falling in love were two sides of the same coin? At least for the sort of person *she* was?

And now here she was, with the train pulling in to London and a magazine in front of her that was a cruel reminder of how stupid she had been.

Lucy had picked the magazine up at the newsstand at the station because she had got there way too early and had forgotten to pack her usual reading fodder for the journey. It was one of those weekly glossies that she never usually read, but she had found herself leafing through it with considerable enjoyment until she came to the centre spread, which was essentially a series of photos taken at the latest prominent society do—in this case the glitzy opening of an art gallery in Canary Wharf. Everyone in the pictures seemed to have a drink in their hand, and were schmoozing with other well-known personalities.

She hadn't expected to see Gabriel in those pictures. He wasn't just in one picture. He was in eight pictures. It was as if the cameraman hadn't been able to get enough of him.

As the train stopped and everyone began the unsteady process of gathering their belongings, eager to clear off, Lucy cast a fulminating glance at the magazine she had stuffed in the netting on the back of the seat in front of her. The instant she had seen those photos she had determined to put them out of her mind. She and Gabriel were not tied to one another. He was a free man and could do whatever he wanted to do!

And yet…

She fetched the magazine back from the resting place to which it had been consigned, hating herself for her masochistic weakness.

It was cold outside.

Gabriel had been remarkably consistent in making sure never to arrange anything that might interrupt one of their weekends. Lucy took a pull-along case with her clothes inside and returned to her house with every stitch of clothing still in it. Few women had ever stayed the night with him, he had admitted early in their relationship. She was the exception. Lucy knew better than to take advantage of that by leaving a wardrobe of clothes behind her, and nor did she want to. She had changed from the young innocent he had first met. Now she had a much more highly developed sense of self-protection.

She glanced at the magazine in her hand and winced. Clearly not *that* developed, or she wouldn't now be feeling as though her heart was forcibly being ripped from her body.

Usually Gabriel accompanied his driver to meet her at the station, and the thrill she felt whenever she laid eyes on him lounging against his car, waiting for her, had not diminished over time. Right now she needed to give herself a few moments to get her thoughts together, so she headed for the nearest bench and sat on it while the crowds surged around her. Against her will, she flattened out that horrid page on her lap and stared.

Gabriel, with the obligatory champagne flute in one hand and a sultry, sexy brunette laughing up at him. The same sultry, sexy brunette was in all the pictures with him, in a tight, tight dress and high, high heels. She had lots and lots of rippling dark hair, and what really shook Lucy was how *good* they looked together. Dark, arresting beauty matching dark, arresting beauty. The camera loved them both.

Had Gabriel complied so willingly to her insistence that they only meet at weekends because it suited him that way? She couldn't get her head round the thought that there might be another woman in his life. Surely she couldn't be so mistaken about someone's personality? She hated herself for even thinking that she was sharing him with someone else, that she couldn't trust him, and yet…

He didn't care about her. Not really. He certainly didn't envisage any sort of long-term relationship. He had made it clear from the very beginning that he wasn't a man into commitment, that he was repulsed by needy, clingy women…

And for a man who was not emotionally tied in any way wouldn't it be easy and tempting to take what was on offer and see no problem in it? Wouldn't exclusivity be something that just didn't exist in his world the way it did in hers?

He was waiting impatiently for her outside, but as soon as he spotted her slight figure emerging from the station Gabriel felt himself relax. He had to suppress a smile at the sight of her waterproof jacket flapping in the wind.

She had indulged in a couple of new items of clothing over the months they had been seeing each other, but she never looked truly comfortable in anything that was fancy. She had proudly donned this new jacket for him a couple of weeks ago, and he had refrained from telling her that the fashionable length and the very attractive belt that she could pull tight to accentuate a waist that was a handspan were sadly diminished by the multitude of pockets—most of which were unnecessary—that turned the jacket into a fashion disaster. When she told him where she bought it he had tried not to wince.

The truth was that the more he saw her, the less he could picture her in anything but clothes in which she felt comfortable—although that didn't mean that he intended giving up on trying to buy her a new wardrobe. The most she would allow him to buy for her was a meal, and even then he always got the feeling that she would rather be staying put or, when it had been warmer, dragging him to picnics in the park, where she'd insisted on getting him on a bike before enjoying lunches she'd enthusiastically prepared herself, despite his protests that he could have the whole thing fully catered—right down to bringing a butler to help.

'You're late. I was beginning to get worried.'

Lucy looked vaguely up at him and saw a laughing man with a champagne flute in his hand and a sexy brunette at his side.

'I…I thought I'd forgotten something on the train and I had to dash back inside to have a look.'

'And had you?' He couldn't wait. He tipped her face up and kissed her with a distinctly uncool lack of restraint.

Every single thought instantly flew out of Lucy's head. Her body reacted as it always did—with a surge of pure, undiluted longing.

'You have no idea how much I've been wanting to do that,' Gabriel said gruffly.

And have you done that? was Lucy's thought. *With another woman? A dark-haired curvy woman with huge breasts and big hair...?*

She didn't want to be thinking these thoughts. She desperately wanted to be the liberated, carefree woman he thought she was—a woman who was as uninvolved as he was, apart from the sex angle—but the thoughts still kept filtering through her brain.

'I'd planned on taking you to one of the top restaurants in the country.' He opened the door and then settled down in the back seat alongside her, leaving his driver to deal with her overnight bag. 'But I'm thinking that a night in might be altogether more enjoyable.'

He couldn't keep his hands off her. Once or twice he

had paused to ponder this interesting phenomenon, because no woman had had that effect on him before, but his pondering never lasted longer than a few seconds. He was well trained in only accepting the facts that fitted in with his life plan.

'I think I'd prefer to eat out,' Lucy told him with a forced smile. 'But not at one of those restaurants with fancy menus and dishes with names I have to ask the head waiter to translate.'

'It's their job. They don't mind.' He grinned at her. 'In fact, it probably makes their day when someone asks them to explain in English what there's no need to say in French.'

'Except no one does, do they?' Lucy muttered, trying and failing to drag herself out of the gloomy vortex into which her thoughts were heading. She laboured the point, her face averted because one look at him and she would be reduced to drowning all over again. 'I mean the people who go to restaurants like those all *know* what the stuff on the menu means. They're well travelled. They don't have to ask for help.'

'What's got into you?'

'Nothing's got into me. I'm just saying.'

'Where would you like to go?'

'Oh, let's just stay in,' she conceded in an abrupt turnaround, because even though she was busily lecturing herself on the stupidity of saying anything—anything *at all*—about those pictures in the trashy magazine she had only glimpsed *accidentally*, in her heart she knew that she would. And a scene in a restaurant would be much more embarrassing than a scene inside his house.

Although restaurants weren't furnished with king-sized beds and baths that could comfortably hold two…

Restaurants also didn't come with scope for her falling into his arms at the slightest opportunity.

Like right now, when he was lightly tickling her wrist on that very sensitive bit that he knew she loved. She couldn't move her hand any more than a chained man could run a marathon.

'Good,' Gabriel said with satisfaction. 'It's been a long week, and I'm in urgent need of just the kind of relaxation only you can provide.'

'It's always sex with you, isn't it, Gabriel?'

'Okay. So now I'm thinking that there's something wrong. Did that fool deliver the wrong plant order?'

'No, that was all fine.' It was brought home to her just how much he knew about the daily workings of her life. He often telephoned, and she would chatter merrily away. She loved the sound of his voice, and yet…how much did *she* know about the daily workings of *his* life? She definitely hadn't known about any openings of art galleries!

'Then do you want to tell me what's bugging you, or shall we go round and round in circles till we get to my place?' Whatever was on her mind, Gabriel was supremely confident that he would be able to sort it out. She had a gratifying respect for what he said, just so long as he didn't touch on the subject of her attire.

'I'm just tired.'

'Easily sorted. I have just the remedy for that.' He shut the partition between himself and his driver and turned to her.

'Gabriel, no! You can't…people can see right in!'

'It's dark outside. An advantage of the days getting shorter. And we're not stuck in traffic.'

God, he wanted her. It was the same every weekend. He just couldn't wait. But never before had he felt the overwhelming need to touch her before they'd even made it to the house. He peeled aside the lapels of her coat and slipped his hand underneath the various layers of thermal vest and jumper to tease his way under the stretchy bra.

'I loathe it when you wear a bra,' he growled softly.

'I thought you loathed it when I went without one....' She curled her fingers into his dark hair and rested back as he pushed up her clothes and the bra in one easy movement, so that one breast offered itself to his searching mouth. When he latched onto her nipple with a low moan of contentment she couldn't stop herself from wriggling lower in the seat.

It was mind-blowingly erotic to watch him through lowered lashes as he suckled hard on her nipple, drawing it into his mouth and sending piercing arrows of pleasure through her. As always, just with one touch, her body was screaming out for more.

As the car purred into the cul de sac he reluctantly detached himself from her breast, neatly pulled her clothes back down and grinned.

'You taste like heaven....' This was so much more effective than talking sometimes.... 'One of these days we're going to go on a drive, park in an isolated lay-by somewhere and I'm going to make love to you very thoroughly in the back seat of this car.... I'm going to start with your mouth, and then I'm going to move to your breasts, and by the time I get to...'

'Shh!' Her face was bright red, and the worrying thoughts that had been her companions on the train were temporarily displaced by images of him doing those things to her in the back seat of his car.

'Let's get you inside. I'll order something for us to eat later.'

He was an irresistible force, and she was as powerless in the face of it as a matchstick being swept along on a wild, torrential river.

By now she was familiar with his house and no longer over-awed at its size and opulence. She knew its layout intimately, and so she knew where they were going as soon as he branched off to the left.

His study was one of the rooms in his house that she loved the most. Unlike the rest of the rooms, most of which she privately found lacking in soul, the study was warm and decorated in deep colours. The Persian carpet was all faded rich reds and burgundies, the velvet drapes that pooled on the ground were of a similarly dark maroon colour, and the desk was a huge mahogany antique. To one side a low, comfortable sofa had been positioned for those times, Gabriel had told her, when he wanted to work through the night with only occasional interruptions for sleep.

They made it to the sofa in a state of semi-undress, having left a trail of discarded clothing *en route.*

'We'll have to dispense with the foreplay just this once,' Gabriel husked. 'I can't wait.'

His impressive steel erection pressed against her thigh as he quickly disposed of her pants.

Lucy moaned her assent. These were the only times when she saw him stripped of his self-control and she loved it. She loved the heady feeling of knowing that she and only she had insight into the real man behind the cool mask of power and assurance.

But was she really the only one privileged to see that?

That sudden disconcerting thought came like a fast ball out of nowhere and hit her for six—but already he was edging her legs apart and the thought was disappearing as quickly as it had come.

He drove into her and she cried out with pleasure. When he withdrew to ram into her with yet more force, sinking his shaft to the very hilt, she crooked her legs over his back and was carried away on a tide of shockingly erotic ecstasy as he kept thrusting, pushing her back on the sofa, pinching her nipples as she arched up to heighten the wild sensations.

She was carried away with primitive, elemental lust. It emptied her head of all thought, swept aside the dimensions of space and time…

Only afterwards, when they had both surfaced from their lovemaking, did the questions begin again, nibbling away at the back of her mind with sharp little rat's teeth.

He was sprawled on the sofa, the very picture of the Lord of the Manor whose needs had been met, and Lucy pushed herself up to clamber over him.

'Where are you going?' Gabriel asked with lazy amusement. He propped himself up on his elbow and savoured her nudity. 'Good luck locating all your clothes. I think if you follow the trail you'll probably get to the first item we discarded when we walked through the front door.'

He reluctantly followed her out of the room, watching as she scooped up underwear in one place, her jeans somewhere else, all the way until she was clutching the last item and heading up the stairs. He thought that she moved like a dancer, lithe and graceful.

Lucy was screamingly aware of his eyes on her behind, and she hurried up the stairs—only to spin round at the top and ask in a rush, 'So…I never asked…how was *your* week?'

The question took him by surprise. 'My week was fine—and yours?' He dealt her a smile of pure amusement.

'You know how my week was. You telephoned and I told you all about it.'

'The business with the plant order…that illustration that's giving you trouble…Martha the landscape gardener who's having an affair with John the other landscape gardener on the team… Oh, yes—so you did…'

'It's all very boring, isn't it?' Lucy sniped back.

Now she felt ashamed that she had flung herself into bed with him when she had all these ugly doubts at the back of her mind. Had she no pride? Could it be undone so easily with a few caresses? She was desperate not to let those pictures get to her, to give him the benefit of the doubt, but was that because she really and truly believed that he would never cheat on her? Or because the thought of having to deal with something that might end up in a place she didn't want scared the living daylights out of her?

'What's got into you?'

Lucy didn't trust herself to answer. She spun round and flew down the marble corridor, with its silk rugs and the perfectly positioned chaise longue, towards his bedroom, where she proceeded to fling her holdall into the bathroom and slam the door behind her, making sure to lock it. Many a time, her bath had been interrupted by him, and they had ended up doing things to each other that would have made her hair curl six months ago. Right now, she just wanted to *think*.

She ran a bath and let her body relax in the bubbles. So she had gone and fallen in love with him, she thought bitterly. Well, she was on a learning curve now, and the first thing she would have to master was the art of not melting the second he laid a finger on her. He would surely be able to talk his way out of the sexy brunette, and he would probably be telling the truth, but from now on she would have to start pulling back. The longer she remained with him, floating in this vacuum where any future together was a subject that was strictly off-limits, the more she would be hurt when they inevitably broke up.

He was clothed and on the bed when she emerged into the bedroom, his dark eyes watchful.

'I'm listening,' Gabriel said bluntly.

'I just think we need to talk.'

'We talk a lot.'

'*I* talk a lot. I tell you all about my dull life at the garden centre. Since when are you *really* interested in plants and flowers and landscape gardeners having flings?' She paced the room, only pausing to throw him a frowning look from under her lashes. She could have added that he wasn't interested in her family…that he had practically banned any talk about that…

'I'm interested because you're interested,' Gabriel said shortly.

'Not good enough, Gabriel. And I don't want to talk to you here.' She hesitated when he continued to look at her coolly, without moving a muscle. He would be hating this—but tough. 'There's something I want to show you.'

'Just tell me where this is leading, Lucy, and spare me the dramatics.'

'I'm not being dramatic.' She felt like a piece of elastic, stretched to breaking point, and it was really hard looking at him because she was so aware of how weak she was in his company. She went to her holdall, in which she had stuck the glossy magazine, and pulled it out. The backs of her eyes stung with unshed tears as she smoothed out the centre spread and walked over to the bed with it.

'What's this?' Gabriel slung his legs over the side of the bed and walked over to the window with the magazine.

She was fighting to hold back tears. He could see that. There was nothing he disliked more than a weeping woman, and he fought off the unusual temptation to pull her to him and let her cry. He realised that he didn't like thinking of her unhappy. She so seldom was. He glanced down at the coloured pictures and then stopped to look a little more carefully at the pictures of him, taken by one of the snap-happy photographers who had been milling at that art gallery like parasites.

'Well?' Lucy was stunned when he casually stretched out his hand to return the magazine to her. 'Aren't you going to say anything?'

'What's there to say?' He threw the magazine onto the chair when she failed to take it and strode towards her. 'Since when have you started reading rubbish like that? I'm disappointed. I thought you had better taste.'

'It's not a matter of taste, Gabriel. You're missing the point!'

'And what *is* the point?'

'You never mentioned a word about any art gallery opening! You never said a thing about going there with some…some…woman…'

'I didn't think I had to give you a minute-by-minute explanation of what I do during the week!'

'That's not what I'm saying at all!'

'No? It sounds that way to me,' Gabriel said coolly. He had never tolerated having his movements questioned and he wasn't about to start now. 'Look how worked up you are! Let's go downstairs—get some food, have something to drink. You're making a mountain out of a molehill.' As conciliatory gestures went that was as good as it got—and it was considerably more than he had ever offered any other woman.

Lucy's heart was beating furiously as they went back down the stairs. He hadn't even seen fit to explain those pictures and she was tormented by what his silence on the subject meant. A part of her wished that she had never mentioned anything at all, and she had to will herself into acknowledging that it never paid to duck reality.

She accepted a glass of wine and listened to him in dull silence as he ordered food in from his caterers.

'How am I making a mountain out of a molehill?' she asked shakily. 'Who was that woman? Are you involved with her?'

'That's an outrageous question!'

'No, it's not.' Lucy dug in her heels and stared down at the kitchen counter. She was grasping the stem of her wine glass so tightly that it might shatter. 'It's a perfectly normal question, Gabriel, and you're blind if you don't see that.'

She raised troubled deep-green eyes to him and he was skewered to the spot. How *dare* she question his integrity? He absolutely refused to be buttonholed into an explanation about nothing!

'We're supposed to be going out together…' Lucy forged ahead in the face of his ominous silence. 'And yet you can't even tell me who that woman is—or else you won't…'

'I refuse to explain myself and that's the end of the matter.'

'Does that mean that you'd prefer not to have an exclusive relationship?'

'No comment.'

'In other words you wouldn't mind if *I* decided to see someone on the side? You wouldn't mind if you discovered that I'd been seeing someone on the side all along? While we've been sleeping together? You'd think that was perfectly all right?'

'Are you?' Gabriel asked in a dangerously soft voice. He was not prepared to yield on this matter even though he was well aware of his double standards—because if he *ever* found out that she had been playing around behind his back…

'If you can't be open and honest and straightforward

with me, then why should I be open and honest and straightforward with you?'

'You knew the kind of man I was before we got into this.' Gabriel raked his fingers through his hair and glowered darkly at her. 'No ties—and that includes not having to justify what I do or don't do. That said, I'm prepared to tell you that the woman in the pictures is just someone I met there. She decided to follow me around, which I found frankly irritating.'

Lucy released a long sigh of relief. But now her thoughts had started moving in another direction, and once embarked on that course they were running wildly out of control.

So he didn't know that woman, and they hadn't slept together. But for him nothing had changed from that very first time they had made love. Emotionally, he had progressed no further—while she had fallen hopelessly in love with him. Seeing him in those shots had brought that home to her very clearly indeed. No ties, no silly dreams. She'd known what she was getting into. With those words he had intended to make it obvious where he stood on her getting any more ideas about questioning his movements.

'So, are we all done with this?'

Lucy shrugged even while she continued to labour the point furiously in her head.

'And I'm taking it that all that nonsense about other men was just your emotions talking...?'

'Yes. I suppose so.'

Gabriel looked at her narrowly. *I suppose so? What the hell did that mean?* Truthfully, though, he knew that she would never fool around behind his back, and he was reluctant to prolong the conversation now that the flashpoint had been averted. In future he would try to be a bit more revealing about what he did from one day to the next. It was a small thing, and it would stop this sort of situation arising again.

'So…dinner in?'

He was back to normal, but Lucy had little appetite for the fabulous meal that was delivered to the door forty-five minutes later. She picked at her sea bass and asked him about the art show—what he had seen, who had been there.

'Next time come with me.' Gabriel had noted her lack of appetite and was prepared to make more concessions. 'You can discover first-hand how deadly some of these things can be.'

'Not my thing. Besides, getting time off work would be difficult.'

'They never give you holidays?' He idly wondered whether it might be a good idea to take her somewhere on holiday. Somewhere hot. Maybe over the Christmas period.

They never spoke about her parents. He had issued a blanket ban on that thorny subject, which could only lead to pointless disagreement, but was she close to them? Would she want to spend Christmas with them? Was that possible? Surely not… After all, what sort of parents gave their daughter the go-ahead to sleep with a man for the sake of a bail-out? Not that he was complaining. She had exceeded expectations when it came to pleasing him. Time was passing and so far the usual stirrings of restlessness that afflicted all his relationships with women were noticeably absent. That said something.

'I would never fit in to those sorts of things, Gabriel. I'm not interested in networking with celebrities and important people I don't know. Life is much safer with my plants.'

'Safer doesn't necessarily mean better.' Gabriel was irritated by her contrary stance. She was usually so obliging, but she had obviously got a bee in her bonnet over the whole art show debacle and was taking her time to regain her easy humour.

Safer means better for me...

That realisation filled her with hot dismay. Not so long ago, when she had kidded herself that she was as nonchalant about their relationship as he was, she had been eager to throw herself into the exciting, dangerous world of being Gabriel Diaz's mistress. She had felt as though for the first time she was really *living.*

Now she was slowly realising that, like some of those wildly beautiful and exotic flowers in the hothouse, Gabriel came with thorns—and his were deadly.

For once she wasn't on red-hot alert for bed. She couldn't face following that train of thought down to its inevitable conclusion so she kept the conversation going, finding more and more things to talk about, until Gabriel looked at her wryly and asked her if she thought she might run out of steam any time soon.

'I can't do this any longer, Gabriel.' She was so shocked at what she had said that she put her hand over her mouth and felt her skin crawl with discomfort.

'Do what? Carry on talking? Then let's go to bed.' He knew it was not what she meant, but he deliberately pretended to misunderstand as an antidote to the sudden flare of panic that had left him feeling a little sick.

'I think we should call it a day.'

'Because of a bloody art show? I told you—I don't even know who that woman was. Was it *my* fault that I couldn't shake her?' When she failed to respond he stood up and began pacing the kitchen. 'You don't mean this.' He leaned over her, caging her in. 'I know you don't. I can see it in your eyes. I could take you right here, right now, if I put my mind to it.'

'I'm sure you could,' Lucy said shakily, 'because I just

lose control when I'm around you. But it wouldn't mean that I'd change my mind. You're not good for me.'

'I've been faithful. I haven't once thought of another woman!'

'I'm really tired.'

'You're blowing one lousy art show out of all proportion!'

'Maybe, but I just want to go to sleep—and not with you. I'd rather sleep in one of the spare rooms.' She suddenly knew that if he was next to her she would just give in again, because she was like an addict—weak. And what he offered was too powerful, too irresistible.

Gabriel thought quickly. She was so rarely emotional. If she needed to sleep on her own—well, he would give her space. She would be fine in the morning. Forcing her to concede now how crazy she was being would most probably backfire on him, whereas she would wake up refreshed in the morning, they would make love, and things would be back on track.

'Your choice.' He hated the thought of it, and even giving in to her request was like swallowing acid.

'I'm sorry.'

'Just get a good night's sleep,' he said quickly, to dispel the finality he heard in her voice. 'Things always look better in the morning, and you'll realise that this is all nonsense. You have nothing to worry about. You're the only woman I want.'

He had to stop himself from physically barring her way as she walked towards the door. He had to tell himself firmly that he was way too disciplined to chase her—and besides, there was no need, because everything would be back to normal in the morning.

CHAPTER SEVEN

GABRIEL STARED OUT of his office window. He was unaware of what was happening outside. There could have been a carnival parade in the streets below for all he cared. Nor was he any more focused on what was happening in his own office. He was aware that he was functioning below par—that he had delegated too many meetings to his directors, had been mentally absent at those meetings he *had* attended.

But the past four days had been tough.

He still couldn't believe that he had been dumped. Yes, Lucy had gone to sleep in a separate room and, yes, she hadn't been in the best of moods, but it had still come as a sickening shock when the following morning, at a little after eight-thirty, he had opened the door to the guest room to find that she and her holdall were no longer in residence.

He should have gone in earlier. It wasn't as though he hadn't been up. He shouldn't have killed time having that shower, giving her a bit more space before he took back control of the situation. In fact, he shouldn't have let her sleep in that guest room at all. If she had been at his side, in his bed where she belonged, she would never have walked out on him!

Hard on the heels of all those frustrating thoughts came the bracing conviction that it was all for the best. All those questions about what he had been up to and with whom… they'd indicated a neediness he despised. He wasn't in the market for being tied down! She had overstepped the boundaries. It was *good* that she was no longer around! He'd had a narrow escape from a woman who had become too demanding. He could move on now. The world was full of women!

He buzzed Nicolette in and she entered with a distinctly wary expression.

'I'll be out for the rest of the day,' Gabriel informed her as he began putting on the coat he had slung over his chair.

'Any instructions?'

'Yes—make sure I'm not disturbed.'

'And what about your meeting with the lawyers from Martins?'

Gabriel looked at her impassively. 'Rearrange. Just make sure I get no calls. If some of these guys can't handle emergencies in my absence then they don't deserve the ludicrously over-inflated salaries they're being paid.'

'When will you be back?' Nicolette hoped that he would take as long as he saw fit and return in less of a foul mood. Walking on eggshells was beginning to get trying.

'I'll be back when I'm back. I'll pick up my voicemail and my emails but I'm counting on you to make sure no one gets through to me.'

For the first time in four days Gabriel was beginning to feel good. Hell, he was well rid of any woman who started trying to tie him down, but damn if she was going to get away with leaving without an explanation that made sense! He'd treated her fairly, hadn't he? More than fairly, in fact, and no one could deny that she had come with a price on her very pretty head. Had he forced her into a deal against her will? No. The second she had told him that she was a virgin he had been the perfect gentleman and had backed off, *still* sticking to his half of the bargain and bailing out her thieving father.

It incensed him to think that his magnanimity had been repaid with her walking out on him without even so much as the courtesy of a note!

It made complete sense that he should want to drive down to Somerset and demand a full explanation face-to-face…the explanation that she had obviously been too cowardly to provide when she had chosen to slink out of his house, *out of his life*, without a backward glance!

There was a bounce in his step as he left the building half an hour later, and he was positively relaxed once in his car, with the radio on, his mobile switched off and his driver given the day off to do whatever he liked to do. Experiment with food, if Gabriel's memory served him right.

He had no intention of taking Lucy back, even if she begged. No, he would just demand an explanation for her irrational behaviour, give her a robust piece of his mind and then he would leave—although the thought of her begging was distinctly satisfying, and it pleasurably occupied his mind for a great deal of the journey.

Lucy locked her front door behind her with a sinking heart. She had dragged out her chores for as long as she possibly could, including walking Freddy. She had also cooked a dessert to take to her parents, and wasted time decorating it with pointless swirls of cream that she knew they would both scrape away for health reasons.

But now she couldn't put off the moment any longer. They had asked her over to dinner and there were things that needed to be said. Including…

She glanced down at her finger, where the tawdry engagement ring she had purchased the weekend before gleamed accusingly in the darkness.

It was only right and proper that a situation that had commenced in a welter of little white lies should end the same way.

Her parents had been pleased when she had begun seeing Gabriel. It hadn't crossed their minds that their relationship was one that was travelling down a one-way street, and she had been loath to break it to them. Why destroy their illusions? she had asked herself guiltily. Now, in retrospect, she could see that she had been nurturing a little seed of hope that had whispered *Who knows? Maybe something will come of it...*

But over the past few weeks they had begun to express curiosity as to where it was all going. They had tactfully skirted round the acknowledgement that she was sleeping with him, but had suggested, with an equal amount of tact, that surely a decent, honourable man who was sleeping with their precious daughter would by now be showing some concrete sign that he was serious about the relationship....

So she had got herself engaged.

Lucy dithered in the cold and then took a deep breath as she began walking towards her car.

Why had she told her parents that she was engaged? It had been just another crazy decision in a long line of crazy decisions that had begun the moment Gabriel Diaz had entered her life. But it had calmed their anxieties and that had been good—because Lucy lived with the constant unspoken dread that her mother might end back up in hospital if she became too stressed or anxious.

Well, now she had to unengage herself, and she wasn't looking forward to the process.

She was about to climb into the driver's seat when a car came pelting down the lane that led to her cottage.

She could hardly make out the shape of it because the

lane was quite unlit. It screeched to a halt, blocking her in, and her mouth fell open just as she was about to lay into whatever maniac was behind the wheel.

Even in the dark it was impossible to miss Gabriel's long, lean silhouette as he slung himself out of his sports car and strode towards her. He was danger personified and Lucy fell back, her mouth still inelegantly open in shock.

'What are you doing here?' she whispered as he neared her.

She had spent the past few days hoping and praying that he would chase her, and then hoping and praying that he wouldn't, and now that he was actually here, standing in front of her like a dark, avenging angel, her bones felt as though they had turned to water.

'You walked out on me.' Five words spoken with grim, merciless accusation.

'That was *days* ago....' Except, having blurted that out, Lucy now realised how plaintive it sounded—as though she had been expecting him to be in touch sooner. 'And... and I don't want you here...I'm...just about to go out, as you can see...'

'You're not going anywhere till we've talked.' He glanced across to his car. 'Unless, of course, you can walk to your destination. In which case, you'll have me for company all the way.'

'You can't do that! And there's nothing to talk about. I said everything I had to say.'

'Why did you run away? Couldn't you face me?' He strolled up to the front door and waited for her.

She couldn't get anywhere—not unless she could work a minor miracle with her car and three-point turns.

Lucy had broken out in a fine film of nervous perspiration. How could she explain that she hadn't been able to face him because he had such a powerful hold over her?

That in her heart she suspected that he could talk her into doing whatever he wanted, however strong her objections? That she had to protect herself because she had been stupid enough to fall in love with him?

'I have to make a call,' she muttered, her nerves jumping all over the place as she pushed open the front door and hurriedly made a hushed call to her mother, telling her that she might be a little late for dinner.

'Something's come up,' she whispered *sotto voce*, while Gabriel breathed down her neck. She concluded the call before her mother could launch into a series of worried questions.

'You bet something's come up,' Gabriel ground out as he followed her into the sitting room. 'Who were you on the phone to?'

'No one.' She spun round to face him. She did her utmost to take a determined stance, but the second her eyes fell on that magnificently, darkly brooding face all her determination seemed to turn to dust and her mouth went dry.

Gabriel picked up on her every emotion with the accuracy of a jungle cat sensing its prey. He shoved his hands into his pockets and strolled towards her, noting the way she had frozen to the spot, the way her pupils were dilated, the pallor of her face that made that little line of freckles across the bridge of her nose really stand out.

She had flown out of his house under cover of darkness but he could still take her right here, right now, if he wanted to. It was something he just *knew*.

Did he want that, though? Hadn't he driven down here for the explanation he deemed justified? Wasn't that the only reason? He certainly wasn't into chasing women who dumped him—not that it had ever been known to happen before.

'Interesting,' Gabriel drawled. 'And do you often make hushed phone calls to *no one*?'

'I haven't got time to stand here and listen to you being sarcastic, Gabriel.'

Her hand was shaking as she lifted it to brush her fingers through her hair. Which was when he saw the ring. Although, because it was the last thing he expected to see, it took a few seconds for the image to compute and for the information to be transmitted to his brain.

And then every nerve in his body froze. His very clever, always fast-functioning mind, seemed to shut down. His skin crawled with a growing onslaught of ugly suspicion that coalesced into white-hot fury.

A lifetime's worth of discipline slammed into place. He reached out and caught her fluttering hand in his.

'What's this?'

'Nothing!' She hadn't even thought about the wretched fake engagement ring. She had been so busy trying not to fall apart at the seams that she had completely forgotten about it, but now she stared down at it, scarcely able to breathe.

'Speaking to no one on the telephone and wearing nothing on your finger? Incredible.'

'Gabriel, let me explain…'

'Why bother? I already know what's going on. The last thing I need is a bunch of nasty little lies from you.'

'What do you mean?'

'You've played me for a fool, and no one does that.'

'How? How have I played you for a fool?' Lucy's eyes were round with incomprehension.

'How long has it been going on?'

'Gabriel, I don't know what you're talking about!'

'When did you decide that it would be an idea to use *me* to get the sexual experience you were lacking? That boyfriend of yours walked out on you because you wouldn't go the final distance with him…'

Lucy stared at him in horror. She was mesmerised as much by the seething fury in his black-as-midnight eyes as by the incredible ability of his agile brain to jump to all the wrong conclusions.

Belatedly she realised that the fictitious boyfriend was yet again rising to the surface—which just proved how one small, innocently spoken fib could end up landing you in a lot of trouble.

'You don't understa—'

'Did you think that you could use me as a practice run for…' his voice was wintry cold as he lifted her hand with its gleaming fake engagement ring '…boyfriend number two? It makes sense now, why the virginal maiden didn't take the escape route I offered and chose instead to jump into the sack with me….'

'You've got it all wrong!'

'Was the other man on the scene then? Or did he appear later on? When you had all the confidence you needed to go out into the big, bad world and hook some other poor sap?'

'How dare you?' Shock was giving way to anger. 'Do you know how insulting you're being, Gabriel? Do you *really* think that I'm the kind of girl who could have two men at the same time?'

'How the hell do I know who you are? Did I think that you were the sort of girl to walk out without bothering to leave a note? No. So let's just say that I got it all wrong when it came to sussing you out!'

Where had his cool gone? And how dare she look at him with those big, accusing green eyes as though *he* was the one in the wrong? And how dare his body, his *disci-*

plined body, react to those big green eyes with a disobedient surge of uncontrollable *craving*?

'Was I worth it?' he ground out hoarsely. 'I must have been if you've managed to bag an engagement ring!'

'Oh, why don't you take a closer look at this stupid ring?' Lucy cried.

This wasn't what Gabriel had been expecting. Insincere excuses, out-and-out lies, maybe a robust defence and some heated counter-attack—but why on earth would she be asking him to look at the damned ring?

'Come again?'

'Take a close look at the ring, Gabriel! And tell me what you think!'

Gabriel caught her hand and frowned at the glitzy bauble on her finger.

'I think you could have done better,' he growled.

He flung her hand away and walked to the French doors, through which he stared at the darkened shadows in the garden. He was dimly aware of a dog yapping merrily away from the direction of what he assumed was the kitchen.

'Surely,' he said, turning to look at her coldly, 'I primed you for more than some cheapskate guy who can't even run to a real diamond?'

He could breathe now that she wasn't right there in front of him, close enough for him to give in to the tawdry temptation to reach out and pull her to him and demand whether his competition was better in the sack than he was.

'Are you going to tell me who he is?' Gabriel thought that the second he was in possession of a name he would make sure to hunt the guy out and physically teach him a thing or two. 'Does he know about us?'

'How can you be so *thick*...?' Tears shimmered on her eyelashes and she chewed her lip to hold them back from spilling. 'And what sort of opinion do you *have* of me?'

She glared at him angrily. How could a guy who was so smart be so *stupid*? 'I thought you might know me well enough by now! I'm not *bloody* engaged to someone else! And I *haven't* been sleeping with anyone behind your back! How could you think that I would ever *use* you as…as *practice*…?'

She walked on unsteady legs towards him. She was distantly aware of Freddy yapping from where she had shut him in the kitchen. She was also aware of her telephone ringing and knew that it would be her parents.

'I bought this…this…*idiotic* ring for myself!'

'What? I'm not following you.'

In any other situation Lucy would have burst out laughing, because she had wrong-footed him and it showed in the uncustomary bewilderment on his face.

'I'm engaged to *you*!'

'Don't be ridiculous!'

'Before you start panicking, it's not a *real* engagement. I know that! It's a stupid, *stupid* phoney engagement—just like this stupid, *stupid* phoney ring!' She twisted it round and round on her finger.

Gabriel shook his head and raked his fingers through his hair. He wasn't getting this. On the other hand, he was strangely relieved that there was no other guy on the scene. The relief, indeed, was far greater than the new conundrum facing him.

'I was about to go and have dinner with my parents when you showed up,' Lucy continued grudgingly. 'To tell them that the engagement's off. So you'll have to leave. If I'm not with Mum and Dad in the next half an hour they'll probably fly over here to find out if I'm still alive. They're like that.'

'I'm not going anywhere until I know what the hell is going on, Lucy.'

'Gabriel, *please…*'

'Why would you lie to your parents? Is deception something that runs in your family?'

'Oh, shut up!' She turned away. Her eyes were blurred with tears. She just couldn't speak. Everything was so *wrong.* She felt as helpless as if she had suddenly been caught in a riptide without warning and without a life belt.

Gabriel found that the sight of her crying was the equivalent of having a shard of glass driven through his chest. He loathed the feeling.

'So you're going to see your parents? Fine. I'll come with you. You can explain on the way. And we'll take my car. I don't like the look of that pile of rusting tin in your drive.'

'You *can't* come with me!' Lucy clenched her fists by her sides and glared up fiercely at him. 'Didn't you hear a *word* I've just been telling you? I'm going over there to tell them that it's all over between us! That the engagement's off! You can't just show up with me!'

'As the wounded party, I have every right.' He began moving towards the door. He still didn't know what the hell was going on, but one thing he *did* know. The questions in his head needed answering, and he had no intention of leaving until they were all answered.

Lucy stared at him and hated the familiar stirrings in her body. 'I hate you right now,' she breathed.

'We're wasting time. You don't want your mum and dad racing over here, do you? Far better for us to drive there and talk on the way….' He reached for his car keys and tossed them casually in his hand.

Any qualms he might have had about embarking on this trip—and there had been very few—had all been neatly laid to rest. In fact, he was congratulating himself on a decision well made. Whatever transpired, he would certainly be returning to London without that unsettling shadow lurking over his life, making it impossible for him to function.

'What about the dog?' he asked as she followed him out of the house and slammed the door behind her.

'I stick him in the kitchen when I'm going out,' Lucy replied. 'He's got plenty of food and water and not much he can chew on.'.

'So…' Car started, engine purring, Gabriel turned to her, cool as a cucumber. 'I'm all ears…'

Lucy stared stonily ahead of her, but continuing silence wasn't going to work. Gabriel was as persistent as a dog with a bone. He wasn't going to give up until he had squeezed every ounce of her miserable story out of her and she just refused to care any longer.

Maybe it would be a good thing if he met her parents anyway. Maybe he would see, then, that her father *wasn't* a dedicated criminal who had escaped the hands of justice by the skin of his teeth. And maybe her parents would be able to see *why* she and Gabriel, sadly but inevitably, had had to break off their 'engagement'! They had asked so many times to meet the lucky guy dating their daughter. Now they would see just how far apart she and the 'lucky guy' really were. They would understand *first hand* how two people from two different planets could never make a relationship work!

'My parents are very old-fashioned people…' she began wearily.

Gabriel stifled a hoot of derisive laughter. If she wanted to introduce her story via a sob story that no one in their right mind would believe, then so be it.

'I never told them about…that you had *blackmailed* me into a deal…that you wanted *sex* for money…'

'Just as well,' Gabriel inserted smoothly, 'because you

would likewise have had to confess that you threw yourself at me even when I was prepared to fulfil my side of the bargain and release you from your dirty deal—no sex, just lovely money….'

Lucy blushed furiously, but there was no denying the truth behind that infuriatingly barbed statement of fact.

'I gave them the impression that we were…dating. After a while they began asking questions. They wanted to meet you.'

'They must have been over the moon at the development,' Gabriel murmured mildly. 'The king of bail-outs sleeping with their daughter. I bet they thought that their boat had really docked…'

'You make me so angry, Gabriel. You think you know everything.'

'I've always been good at judging human nature. But, hey, let's not get sidetracked. I'm curious to see where all this is leading.'

'They wanted to know if what we had was going anywhere. I could have told them that it wasn't…' Lucy thought she might expand on this point, just in case he got it into his arrogant head that she had nurtured dreams beyond her reach. She didn't think she could bear the humiliation of him thinking that she had done just that. 'Which would have been the truth. But my mother's health isn't brilliant. She suffered a massive stroke a while back and she's been left with heart problems ever since. Dad and I have done all we can to protect her from stress, and I knew it would stress her out if she thought that we were sleeping together but weren't in any kind of serious relationship…'

'So you decided that you'd better have us engaged and on the road to a happy-ever-after wedding?' He marvelled that she could make her parents sound like two characters from a Disney movie. 'How long have we been engaged?'

'Not long. A week.'

'And now you're about to call the whole thing off…' He was following her directions to her parents' house on autopilot. As tales went, this was the most far-fetched one he had ever heard in his life.

'I just couldn't carry on with us any longer, Gabriel. I'm sorry I didn't leave you a letter, or something, but I honestly didn't see what difference it would make. I'd made my mind up and I didn't think you'd really mind anyway… I know you have a casual approach to relationships…'

'Are we going to hark back to the non-existent sex I was supposed to have with a random stranger who followed me around an art exhibition I didn't want to go to?'

'No,' Lucy interjected hurriedly. 'I'm just saying that I have to break off the fake engagement because I won't be travelling to London every weekend….'

The absence of those visits swamped her. She was staring into a deep, black, bottomless void with no sign of light. It was a suffocating feeling. Maybe if Gabriel wasn't sitting right next to her she would be taking the first steps to recovery, but his presence was overwhelming—a horrible reminder of the empty future awaiting her.

'So what are you going to tell them?' Gabriel asked with interest. He slid his eyes across to her profile. She was the most unpredictable person he had ever known. Maybe that had been part of her fascination. 'I won't be amused if I'm painted as the bad guy.'

'I intend to tell them that we're poles apart and that it's an amicable separation. Take the next left and then the first right and we're there. You don't have to come in with me.' She turned to him impulsively. Forget about her parents meeting him first-hand. Lucy just couldn't envisage Gabriel in her parents' little detached cottage, judging them, believing her father to be a crook despite what she might tell him to the contrary. 'In fact, I'd rather you didn't. You could just drop me at the end of the street and I can make my way there….'

'Won't it be difficult to explain why you've walked to their house? At night? Down these remarkably unlit side roads?'

Lucy leaned back and closed her eyes. She felt thoroughly defeated. How had life become so complicated? The good old days of the garden centre, gossip with her friends, the occasional cinema trip and absolutely *no Gabriel* on the scene seemed like a lifetime ago.

'So you're going to come in, are you?' She looked at him and her breath caught in her throat. He was just so beautiful. *Beautiful*, she reminded herself, and *dangerous*.

'I feel I should, don't you? Considering I'm part of this ongoing drama. Even though I didn't apply for the position.' He slowed the car right down and pulled over, leaving the engine to idle.

'What are you doing?' She was suddenly inexplicably panicked.

'You're as jumpy as a cat on a hot tin roof. Is that because you're scared at how your parents are going to take the bad news?'

Lucy could have told him that next to his being in the car here the *drama* with her parents and her concern over how they would take the news ran a very poor second. The minute Gabriel was around everything and everyone faded into the background, and it was no different now, even though she had broken up with him. Developing a tough shell to protect herself felt as hopelessly out of reach as a trip to the moon.

'Of course I am!' she agreed quickly. 'You would be too if you knew them. They're not what you think they are.

But I don't know why I'm bothering to tell you this when I know you won't listen to a word I have to say anyway.'

'Well, soon I'll find out for myself what they're like, won't I?'

The house he pulled up in front of moments later was a comfortable detached bungalow, not in the least flashy—but then the man had been caught before he'd had had time to really dip his hands in the till.

This was a slice of Lucy's life he had deliberately sealed off into a closed compartment. She had attempted on several occasions to open up a dialogue on the subject of her father and he had very quickly terminated the conversation. He had felt no necessity to remind himself of her highly questionable background. After a while she had given up. Now, he felt as though the missing bits of her were quietly slotting into place to form a complete picture. Did he want that? Well, he certainly didn't have much of a choice, because he wasn't about to drive off into the distant horizon, which was what *she* wanted.

Gabriel killed the engine and turned as he felt her small hand lightly rest on his arm.

'This was such bad timing,' Lucy murmured. 'One day later and you would never have known about…any of this….'

'True…but then perhaps fate decreed that I shouldn't miss my own engagement….'

'Promise me you won't say anything?' Lucy pleaded in an urgent undertone. 'I mean, just take the lead from me. I'll get us out of this, and then you can get back to London and forget any of this ever happened.'

Gabriel refrained from saying that that seemed a very tall order.

'And please try and…be kind to my dad….'

Gabriel wouldn't dream of being *kind* to anyone who

had stolen from him. He looked at her anxious face and shrugged. 'What your father did is history, and I have no intention of dredging up the past. Besides…' he shot her a slow smile that made her suddenly breathless '…I'd be the first to admit that I got more than my money's worth….'

Lucy knew that he was going to kiss her. It was as if somewhere deep inside her she could connect to him on an unspoken, elemental level. She gave a soft little moan of protest and surrender and was ashamed to find herself clinging to him as his lips covered hers savagely, fiercely demanding. She was leaning over to him and the familiar heat was making her giddy….

She pulled back when sanity reasserted itself and he looked at her sardonically.

'Okay,' Lucy blurted out before he could say anything, 'so you're an attractive man…' She could hardly breathe, and every bit of her body wanted this forbidden experience to carry on. 'But it still doesn't work for me. I…let's just get this over with and then you can leave and we can both get on with our lives….'

CHAPTER EIGHT

NICHOLAS AND CELIA ROBINS opened the door on the first ring of the bell and Lucy beamed so broadly at them that her jaw began to ache. She would be calm, relaxed, in control and cheerful at this amicable end to a relationship that wasn't meant to be. She had instructed Gabriel to lurk to one side, out of sight, to give her an opportunity to announce his entrance.

She was still smarting from his kiss. Her lips felt swollen. She prayed that her parents wouldn't spot that when, very shortly, she would be breaking the sad news that their dreams of marrying her off were at an end. The demise of an engagement was never preceded by the fiancé kissing his woman until her skin burned.

'We've been worried!' Her mother's thin face still wore signs of anxiety.

'Mum, I'm an hour late. Not even that!'

'You know what your mother's like, pet. If you're five seconds late she's wondering if you've had an accident and complaining about the state of your car.'

As usual they were both formally dressed, her mother in a pair of slacks and a pink jumper, her father in grey trousers, a blue jumper and a tie. She had frequently tried to introduce them both to the concept of comfortable jogging pants and sweaters but had never been able to make much headway. They were both in their sixties and old habits, as they always smilingly told her, died hard. Now they were ushering her in, already beginning to tell her an anecdote about a fox that had taken a liking to their garden, asking her opinion on whether it was a pest or a pal of sorts. She stopped them.

'I...I...er...there's someone I'd like you to meet... Gabriel's here....' It all came out in an embarrassed rush and she winced at the pleasure that spread across her mother's face.

She had no idea how to proceed. The fact that Gabriel was around changed everything. She'd had her little speech planned, had worked out what she intended to say. Did she trust him to follow her lead, as she had instructed? Did Gabriel Diaz *ever* listen to instructions or follow leads?

While she frantically debated all possible scenarios he was already edging himself through the door behind her, and all of a sudden she was swept along into an impromptu situation where he was being pulled inside and led to the sitting room and she loitered behind like a spare part.

She hardly dared cast her eyes in his direction. What was he thinking? That he had stepped into his worst nightmare? Being forced to meet the man who had defrauded his company? Father of the woman who had ditched him? How much worse could it get for him?

She traipsed into the sitting room in a daze, to find him seated and with a drink being pressed into his hand.

The bungalow, whilst spacious for two, and certainly having benefits from its one floor because her mother had no need to tackle stairs while she was still recovering from her stroke, was small. Lucy thought that the entire bungalow would fit into the downstairs of Gabriel's massive London townhouse.

She knew that if she didn't get a grip very soon the conversation would run away and it would be difficult to rein it back. She had told Gabriel to follow her lead. She fancied he must be cringing at the ongoing assumption that they were an engaged couple. But before she could launch into explanations and apologies her mother was tugging her towards the kitchen and whispering that they should *'leave the boys alone for a little while...your father would like a quiet word with Gabriel...'*

'You should have warned us that Gabriel would be coming!' was the first thing her mother said once they were in the kitchen and out of earshot. 'I've only done something simple for us. Beef pie. I know it's your favourite, but it's really not fancy at all. Plus there's no champagne in the house!'

'Mum, please stop fussing,' Lucy said awkwardly. 'Um…champagne won't be necessary anyway…' Once again she bitterly regretted the lies that had thrown her into this situation.

'Of *course* champagne's necessary, darling. Not only to celebrate, but because we're both so grateful for Gabriel's generosity… Not many employers would have looked so kindly on your father's situation. In fact, I think that's what they're talking about now. Your dad contemplated writing him a letter, but I told him it would be so much better to thank Gabriel face-to-face. He would have gone up to London to see him personally, but when you two started dating he thought he would wait until he visited. Neither of us guessed for a minute that he would be visiting as our future son-in-law!'

'Well, here's the thing, Mum…'

But Celia Robins was in full flow. She ordered her daughter to peel more carrots and to fetch a recipe book, because she could remember seeing a recipe with carrots that would elevate them from boiled with butter to something a little fancier—and what about the crockery? Should they get their best out or stick to casual?

'I'm as nervous as anything,' she confided at one point, 'but I can tell that he's a wonderful person. Kind-hearted. And good-looking, too!'

Lucy had to stop herself from bursting into laughter. The truth was that her mission seemed to be fraying miserably at the edges and her mother had taken up her pen and asked where to sign to become a full-time member of the Gabriel Diaz fan club!

'Look, Mum…there's really no need to go out of your way. In fact, maybe you'd like to sit down for what I have to tell you…'

'Sit? *Now?* When I'm in the middle of these carrots?' She sat. 'You're not pregnant, are you, darling?' Celia Robins went a deep shade of pink. 'These things happen. Of course they do. I just want to say that your dad and I will be here for you….'

'Mum! Of course I'm not pregnant! Look…I know you're very excited about this…um…engagement thing… but I've taken a step back in the past few days and, well… I've had to be realistic…'

She couldn't quite meet her mother's eyes. Instead she sought inspiration from the kitchen clock, the old-fashioned range cooker, the pine table, the little row of spices in bottles neatly lined up on the shelf her father had put up only a year ago.

'There are loads of differences between me and Gabriel….'

'Opposites attract,' her mother said promptly. 'It's a cliché, but it also happens to be true.'

'Yes, well…' Lucy cleared her throat and looked at her mother with what she hoped was an expression of sincere regret. 'It's not just that we come from two completely different worlds…'

'Are you talking about…*money*?'

'There's that,' Lucy said cautiously. 'I mean, Mum, you should see his house. It's huge. It's full of silk rugs and expensive paintings…'

'I didn't raise you to be concerned about things like that,' Celia admonished her daughter gently.

'And I'm not! But it's all symptomatic of the bigger differences between us.' Lucy sighed. 'I mean, he's a sophisticated, wealthy man. He's good-looking, clever, urbane… In comparison I'm just a simple country girl who has problems when it comes to menus in foreign languages…'

'I've told you that you should never be concerned about that!'

Lucy and her mother both looked up in surprise to see Gabriel lounging in the doorway, dwarfing the kitchen and filling it with his indefinable *presence.*

He strolled forward and placed his hands firmly on Lucy's shoulders. She smiled weakly, rested one hand over his and gave it an over-firm squeeze to remind him that *she* was supposed to be in charge of the break-up conversation with her parents.

'Your daughter seems to think that there's something shameful in asking a waiter to translate a menu, even though I've told her often enough that it's their job,' he said, and bent to feather a kiss on her neck.

Lucy stiffened in confusion but maintained the rictus grin on her face.

'It's flattering to know that you think so highly of me… you should say it more often. A man likes to hear these things…'

He moved round so that he was looking at her. With all four of them now piled into the kitchen Lucy was beginning to feel claustrophobic. She knew she was perspiring. She desperately wanted to know what was going on—but now the meal was being brought to the table and everyone was chatting…

Exhausted from the effort, she finally threw in the towel and announced that she was tired.

'Long week,' she muttered vaguely. 'All sorts of heavy-duty lifting at the garden centre because Pete and Jake are both on holiday.'

Only when they were safely out of the house and in his car did she turn to Gabriel—but he spoke before she could open her mouth.

'I feel I owe you something of an apology.' He started the engine and the powerful sports car slowly pulled away from the drive and into the street outside.

'Sorry?' Like a helpless moth drawn to a flame she stared at him in the darkness, drinking in the hard angles of his face.

'It's possible that I may have jumped to certain conclusions regarding your father's character. Don't get me wrong, in no way do I condone theft of any kind, but that said, your father was…er…somewhat emotional about what he did and why he did it.'

'Oh?'

'In fact, tearful might be a more accurate description…'

'You hate tears.'

'That's perfectly true, but it was obvious that his regret is sincere. He explained about your mother's illness at the time, and his desperation.'

'He wasn't thinking straight. I could have told you all that if you had given me half a chance, Gabriel.'

'It's not in my nature to give credence to sob stories. I've learnt from experience that anyone can rustle up a heartwarming tale of woe if they think there's a pot of gold to be gained at the end of it.'

'You are so cynical.'

'And yet open-minded when it comes to admitting that I may have made a mistake.' Gabriel glanced across at her. She was as rigid as a plank of wood.

Lucy grudgingly admitted to herself that there was an element of truth to that. In the time she had known him she had come to realise that underneath the ruthless demeanour was a fair-minded guy who did all sorts of things no one would ever have guessed just by looking at him. He was a generous contributor to charity, and respected by all the people who worked for him—Nicolette included. She had told Lucy in passing that the profit-related bonuses awarded to his employees, from the bottom up, were second to none in the City. He made generous donations to a dogs' home because, he had confided in one of the rare moments when his vulnerability had made her love him all the more, he had always wanted to have a dog. Of course he had never had the chance as a boy, and now he just travelled too much for the responsibility.

'Well, I'm really happy that you've heard Dad's side of the story…but that's not what I wanted to talk to you about.'

'No?'

'You said that you'd let me take the lead in this whole business….'

'You mean the phoney engagement that's encouraged your mother to start talking with the vicar and buying bridal magazines for tips on how to hold the perfect reception?'

'She hasn't?' Lucy blanched. 'But I only told her this… this…'

'Outrageous lie…?'

'…a week ago!'

'Excited parents can be fast movers. Your father confided that he had seen a formal black suit on sale in the local department store…he was tempted to buy it… My thoughts here are that this engagement is just a formality, with the marriage due any second now—at least as far as your parents are concerned…'

'You're making this stuff up!'

'No, I leave the fabrications to you.' But he was strangely lacking in fury at this unexpected development. He decided that the creative way to play it would be simply to go along for the ride and see where it led him.

'This is *terrible.*' Lucy's voice wobbled. 'I never thought…'

'Hoist by your own petard, is the expression that springs to mind…'

'Well, you didn't make things any easier,' Lucy was constrained to point out. 'I told you to leave all the talking to me. I was going to break it to Mum in the kitchen that it was all over…'

'Because you're just a simple country girl and I'm such a devilishly good-looking, sexy, sophisticated man of the world…well-versed in the art of reading complicated menus…'

He could see her cottage approaching. For the first time he wondered what she must think of his townhouse, with its *über*-expensive furnishings and its ultra-modern feel. Less than impressed, he surmised. So different from all the women he had ever gone out with. Sure, she had oohed and aahed in all the right places, but this country cottage was what she was unashamedly all about. He thought he might like to see that garden centre of hers, meet those people she worked with. She had told him enough about them over the months.

'You realise that I'm going to have to stay the night with you?' Gabriel said gravely as he pulled up outside the cottage. He swung round to face her. 'We still have a conversation to finish, and it's far too late for me to contemplate driving all the way back to London….'

'Yes, well…' she stammered.

'But…' Gabriel held up one hand to interrupt her, '…you needn't fear that I'm going to make a nuisance of myself. You can point me in the direction of the spare room….'

'It's called the sofa in the living room, and you might have Freddy for company. If he knows that you're in the house and sleeping in the living room he'll make sure he informs you that the kitchen isn't good enough for him.'

'I like dogs. You know that.'

Freddy, released from the kitchen, bounded out like a bat out of hell. After a few seconds of astonishment at seeing a new face, he proceeded to demonstrate all the ways he had of enlisting Gabriel as a new friend. Gabriel, returning the favour, didn't seem to care about getting his hands and face licked. Nor did he care about the paw prints all over his expensive designer clothes.

From the sidelines, Lucy watched—hating him for being there and sending her into disarray, and loving him for being there because, as always, he was a sight for sore eyes.

He looked up when she offered to get him a cup of coffee, but it was a while before Freddy calmed down and reluctantly agreed to take his favourite spot in front of the fire, where he was asleep within minutes.

'Your father went into some detail about your mother's health.' Gabriel relaxed back on the sofa and glanced at his surroundings for the first time since he had entered the cottage. There was a higgledy-piggledy charm to the room, with photos in frames, lots of plants and flowers in rustic pots and vases, three small prints of old movie posters, and a big basket by the open fireplace, in which wood had been placed in readiness for when the weather turned cold. The furniture was dated, but comfortable.

'She's never fully recovered,' Lucy admitted. She had taken up position in the comfy chair by the fire, legs tucked under her—a good vantage point from which to observe Gabriel, who now sprawled on the sofa, one arm stretched out along the back, legs crossed ankle on knee, a man at home in his surroundings. It seemed to be a talent he had. He had looked equally at home in her parents' house, even though his own surroundings were so wildly different.

'When you told me that they were old-fashioned I have to admit that I had trouble swallowing it. It didn't quite tally with the embezzler scenario. But I'm seeing your point of view now. And I'm seeing why you plumped for fabrication when your parents started asking questions about us. You thought there would be no harm in taking the path of least resistance.'

'And it was a big mistake. I know that. Now you've been dragged in. I'm very glad that you haven't exploded, but I'm going to set this whole thing straight.'

'And risk your mother going into a meltdown?'

'She won't. I think she's stronger than Dad and I have given her credit for. It's just been so easy to worry… She might be disappointed, but she won't go into a meltdown.'

'And the vicar and the bridal magazines?'

'Why are you *doing* this?' Lucy cried.

In front of the fire Freddy shifted, opened one drowsy eye, and promptly decided that sleep was a better option.

She leapt to her feet and began pacing the room, feverishly trying to keep calm.

'If you want to take the decision to spill the beans and

damn the consequences then go ahead, but I won't be part of that decision. I don't intend to have anyone's hospitalisation on my head,' he said.

'And yet you would have slept like a baby with Dad's incarceration on your head!'

'Different set of circumstances—as you're all too well aware.'

'So what are you saying?'

Gabriel shrugged. 'We could always let this one play out for a little while.'

'Play out for a little while?'

'I looked at your mother over dinner. She's jumpy, anxious, she worries about you, but when she talks about this engagement she lights up like a Christmas tree. I'll be frank: I remember my own mother only in snatches. She wasn't around long enough...and my various stepmothers never left much of a mark. I don't want to be the one who interferes with the relationship you have with her. It's obviously a good one. You're the golden child they had when they were old enough to have given up hoping...'

'Stop trying to make me feel guilty...' But her voice was not quite as convinced as it had been half an hour before.

Was he right? *Had* this engagement given her mother something positive to hold on to? Lucy thought that the vicar and the bridal magazines might be a worrying indication that she had underestimated the value her mother might place on the announcement. And her father had been checking out a *suit*? All that in the space of *a week*? Lucy was appalled.

'Not my intention.'

'We broke up.'

'So we did. Because you overreacted to a picture in a trashy magazine.'

'That's not true!'

'Would you have decided to call it a day if you *hadn't* come across that picture?'

He looked steadily at her and Lucy was suddenly thrown into confusion. Would she? Had seeing that photo been a blessing or a curse? She wanted to ask him why he couldn't just respect her decision. Now he had shown up on her doorstep in a moment of impeccable bad timing and found himself drawn into a drama he hadn't initiated. Could she lay into him because he wasn't reacting the way she had told him to? Because he happened to be in possession of a conscience?

'You should never have shown up here,' she countered weakly. 'I don't even know why you came.'

'I had unanswered questions.'

Dented masculine pride. The same reason he had offered her that deal all those months ago. He didn't love her, and he hadn't charged down to Somerset like a knight in shining armour to try and persuade her to come back. He had come down because, in the end, he just had to win. He had to have the last word.

'If you break off this phoney engagement after a week there's a chance your mother will be more affected than if you leave it a bit longer.'

'I have no idea how you work *that* one out.'

'Leave it longer and it gives you more time to ease her into the notion that we're just not suited.' He shrugged eloquently. 'Of course, having never been in this situation before, I'm only throwing out ideas. Far be it from me to tell you what you should or shouldn't do.'

Lucy looked at him narrowly. Since when had Gabriel ever shied away from telling people what they could or couldn't do? When it came to voicing his opinions he was anything but the shrinking violet.

'People don't suddenly stop being suited to each other in

the space of a few days and hard on the heels of cementing their engagement with a ring.' He eyed her finger with a jaundiced expression. 'And I'd like to say that if that *were* a genuine engagement ring from me it wouldn't look like something straight out of a Christmas cracker.'

'Believe it or not, I didn't put a lot of thought into it. It was the cheapest thing on offer. I was going to try and return it for a refund.'

Gabriel flushed, because that slice of cynicism didn't sit well on her and he knew she had arrived at that place because of him. On the plus side, it never paid to live in cloud cuckoo land. He had done her a favour.

'Sleep on it.' He stood up and stretched. 'It's been a long drive for me. Where can I find some linen?'

Lucy sprang up. So he wasn't going to try anything. Well, *good*! At least her message on that front had been received loud and clear.

She disappeared, to return moments later with an armful of linen. All the stuff she kept for when any of her friends happened to sleep over, if they had had too much to drink and needed a bed for the night.

Once upstairs, she feverishly tried to view the situation from every angle, and from every angle it seemed to be a mess. She was also horribly aware of Gabriel downstairs on the sofa. Grudgingly, she had to admit to herself that he had been pretty sanguine about the whole thing. He had also been generous in his forgiveness of her father's upsetting theft from his company—a complete U-turn from his stance of not wanting to hear a thing about a situation he had condemned as morally inexcusable.

He had made no waves over dinner. He had also given her no opportunity to jump in and announce that their so-called engagement was over, but now, thinking about it, perhaps he was right. One week didn't seem like a long time in which to have decided that their relationship was dead and buried. Leave it a bit longer and she could begin to work on her parents. Disappointment was easier to swallow if it was offered up in stages. A rueful sigh here, a mournful turn of phrase there… Maybe she could even send Gabriel overseas! Perhaps turn him into a world-traveller who couldn't possibly sustain a marriage because he was never in the country!

Her parents would have to agree that she couldn't possibly marry a man who practically lived in Australia! She could even send him to New Zealand, where he could become neighbours with her fictitious boyfriend and his fictitious wife and baby….

Reluctantly she had to concede that she had concocted too many half-truths. Throwing any more into the cauldron would certainly spell disaster.

It was a restless night, and when she awoke the following morning and, having changed into her work clothes, tentatively ventured downstairs, it was to find the house empty. Both Gabriel and Freddy were missing. But her peace was short-lived. No sooner had she buttered her slice of toast than there was the sound of the front door slamming shut and Freddy's excited yelps.

'Hope you don't mind….' Gabriel had clearly not brought a change of clothes, and he was now wet from the fine, grey drizzle outside. 'Thought I'd put in a couple of hours' work and take your mutt for a walk.'

'Shouldn't you be getting back to London?'

'In due course.' He made himself at home in the kitchen, fixing them both coffee and seemingly knowing where everything was to be found.

Lucy followed his movements compulsively. Too well could she recall those weekends at his place, having breakfast together, planning what they would do over the days that had always seemed way too short. Often the breakfast would only be half eaten, because they couldn't keep their hands off one another. On one memorable occasion they had actually made love in the kitchen—fast, hard love that had left her limp and blissfully happy.

Guiltily she averted her eyes, because it no longer seemed appropriate to be staring at him. She had forfeited that right when she had walked away, and she had walked away because she had been stupid enough to fall in love and smart enough to realise that leaving was her only protection.

Except look where she was now!

'You're dressed for work. Why are you dressed for work?' he asked.

'Because that's where I'm going.'

'I'll come with you.'

'Why?'

'I'd like to meet your friends there.' He was already slinging on his coat, giving Freddy one last pat.

'Freddy comes with me. And why do you want to meet my friends?'

'Just showing a natural curiosity about my fiancée's life.'

'I am *not* your fiancée and they don't even know that I'm…we're…'

Gabriel feigned shock. 'So the storyline is purely for the benefit of your parents?'

'That was the plan.'

'You weren't thinking straight when you concocted it, in that case. If the vicar knows, half the village probably does as well. Won't your work friends feel hurt that you didn't share the good tidings with them?'

'This is crazy…' Lucy found herself being gently led

out of the house with Freddy running round in mad circles behind her.

'Crazy in a not very well-thought-out way…' Gabriel murmured.

'You're wet,' Lucy replied inanely.

'Which is why, as soon as we break the good news to your gardening pals, I'm going to get myself down to the nearest shops and buy some clothes….'

'No!' She spun round to face him and felt a little giddy. 'This is all getting completely out of hand.'

'You should have thought of that when you embarked on your well-intentioned charade. You should have realised that your parents weren't to know that they had to keep this engagement a deep, dark secret. Maybe you should have told them that…but I suppose that wouldn't have tallied with true love and romance…'

Lucy fancied she could hear amusement and sarcasm in his voice and she stiffened. 'No. It wouldn't,' she told him shortly. 'They would have found it really hard to understand us falling into bed just for the fun of it. They wouldn't have got it. I'm not your type and you're definitely not mine. I'm not going in your car, Gabriel. I need to take Freddy, and he won't fit in a sports car.'

'In which case, I'll follow you.'

'You don't have to *do* that!' Lucy exploded. 'I suppose I'll have to mention *something,* if Mum's been telling everyone in the village, but if they see you, then they're going to know that it's all a sham!'

'Because…?'

'Because they *know* me, and they *know* that I'd never go for you. At least not as far as getting engaged!'

She stormed over to her car and yanked open the door. She was shaking like a leaf. She hated herself for knowing that, deep down, she would have loved nothing better than to be wearing a *real* ring on her finger, to be secure in a *real* engagement and looking forward to a *real* wedding. She hated *him* for being able to carry on with a farcical engagement because it really didn't trouble him one way or another. He was not emotionally invested. He could afford to look at the bigger picture and have a conscience about the situation. Maybe he felt guilty that he hadn't listened to her in the first place when she had tried to explain about her father. Maybe he felt compassion because he had not had a mother for most of his life and, as he said, he didn't want to be responsible for damaging *hers.* He could *afford* to be as cool as a cucumber while she was a seething mass of conflicting emotions.

Freddy leapt into the back of the beaten-up Land Rover and leaned over the passenger seat, for all the world as if he was truly interested in the scene being played out by the driver's door.

'And something else...' She pulled up the hood of her cardigan and glared at him. She had a driving need to get under his skin. He was just *so* stunning and *so* controlled. He had been a bad choice, but all she could remember when she looked at him was how wonderfully happy he had made her. 'I bet you haven't even thought about the practicalities of what happens if this stupid phoney engagement continues!'

'Explain.' Her eyes were the colour of stormy seas, enormous in her small heart-shaped face. He just had to look at her and his libido went into overdrive. He had stopped trying to find an explanation for that phenomenon. No longer would he beat himself up with the fact that he could still get turned on by a woman who had managed to go against every rule and regulation he had always made sure to lay down about relationships with the opposite sex.

A phoney engagement? This was the stuff of pure horror movies, as far as Gabriel was concerned, and yet, staring down into those sea-green eyes, he could still feel his manhood rising magnificently and inappropriately to the occasion.

'What am I supposed to do at the weekends? Where am I supposed to go?'

'London.' Gabriel shrugged. 'Your visits can taper off in due course.'

'London?' Lucy practically shrieked. 'And what am I supposed to *do* when I'm hiding out in London? Where am I supposed to stay?'

'I'm your so-called fiancée,' Gabriel remarked drily. 'Join the dots.'

'Stay with *you*?'

'Unless,' he murmured, 'you think that I might overstep the mark?'

'I'm not saying that.' Of *course* he wouldn't overstep the mark. His mocking voice was reminder enough that he was over her, that he was simply rolling with the punches.

She resented the fact that she should be grateful to him for not laying his cards on the table when he had visited her parents. He could have told them that it had all been a ridiculous lie—could have left her parents distraught and mistrustful of her for ever.

'Then what other reason could there be not to accept the most obvious solution?'

'So I'd stay with you…?'

'It makes more sense than hiding under your kitchen table and praying that no one comes to the door. I don't *have* to do this, Lucy. Consider it a friendly gesture in recognition of the time we spent together.'

'A friendly gesture…?' Why didn't she like that terminology?

Gabriel spread his hands wide and shot her a slow, toe-curling smile. 'What else? As you've been at pains to point out, we're not each other's type…so there won't be any risk of either of us straying outside the boundaries, will there?'

CHAPTER NINE

THE NEXT FEW WEEKS saw a change in their relationship. Lucy had reluctantly agreed to continue her weekend visits to London, but if she had expected those visits to be awkward and argumentative then she found that she had been mistaken.

Gabriel had moved from being the perfect lover to the perfect host. They went sightseeing. London was explored with the methodical precision of a military campaign. Maps and guidebooks were brought out and consulted. Art galleries were visited. In the evenings—Friday and Saturday—they would eat out in expensive formal restaurants.

Every weekend the guest room awaited her, with the bed neatly made and towels freshly laid out in the adjoining bathroom. They would return from their meals and the second they were in his house he would remove himself to his office. She would be left to contemplate the indifference of the empty bed and the fresh towels.

Gone was any hint of flirtation. Just like that. It was as though they had never slept together. At least insofar as he was concerned. For Lucy, being in his presence and not being able to touch him was agonising. Her fingers seemed poised to stroke his face or rest lightly on his arm, her lips were primed to kiss him, her whole body yearned for the feel of his. She longed for the easy laughter and the teasing. The absence of any physical contact was a continuing wake-up call to the role she had really played in his life. He might have made love to her with consummate passion, but in the end he could detach from all of that as though it had never happened.

He always spoke to her during the week, and she had become accustomed to receiving his calls. They were a guilty pleasure even though there was nothing in them that could be construed as intimate or, as he had said weeks ago, overstepping the boundaries.

After that first flush of realising that she was in love with him, and knowing that her only salvation lay in escape before she could be sucked deeper into the hopeless situation in which she had found herself, Lucy knew that she was sinking fast into a routine that was equally destructive. Buying time before she told her parents that the engagement was off was just a handy excuse. Deep down she knew that what she really needed to do was cut all ties with Gabriel and suffer the withdrawal symptoms, however long it took.

They were no longer lovers, and she gave herself long, scornful lectures on how transitory any feelings he had for her had been, but she still found herself in a state of excitement as Friday rolled round and her trip to London was underway.

He usually sent his driver for her, but today, as she walked out of the station, her heart gave a treacherous little lurch at the sight of him leaning against the car, coolly elegant in a charcoal-grey hand-tailored suit. He must have come directly from work. Her mouth was dry as she walked towards him, shading her eyes from the cold winter glare of the sun.

'What are you doing here?' Lucy asked, surprised.

'Now, now—is that any way to greet your fiancé?'

Dark eyes gave her the once-over, taking in the soft full mouth, the slender body underneath the swinging coat, her very blond, very long hair that trailed over her shoulders and down her back underneath the navy blue woollen hat pulled low to her eyes. He could never get enough of looking at her.

She flushed. This was one of those rare times when she could detect that lazy teasing in his voice that still had the power to make her feel self-conscious.

'Tell me how your trip was,' he encouraged as they settled into the back seat and his driver slowly pulled away from the kerb. 'And tell me what's happening with your friends at the garden centre….'

Lucy sighed. It was way too easy to talk to him. 'They're all fine. The same. I've… I've begun to sow some seeds of doubt, Gabriel…you know… It's been a few weeks, and people are beginning to ask questions…wanting to know when the big day is going to be….' She sneaked a sideways glance at him but couldn't read anything from his expression. 'I've been doing the same with Mum and Dad,' she continued reluctantly. 'They're away this weekend. They left last night and won't be back until Sunday evening. I'm hoping that they'll think about the stuff I said.'

'Which was what, exactly?'

'Oh, just that we hadn't been getting along lately. You know—I harped on about how different we were…. I mean, I didn't lay it on too thick. I just think that it's time for us to really start…ending this. Mum showed me those magazines and tried to drag me along to see the vicar, which I managed to avoid, but it's getting a little tricky and I'm fed up having to pretend. I…I just want to move on with the rest of my life, and I know you want that, too…so…'

'What makes you think that you know what I want?'

'I feel like I'm standing still, and I don't like having to skirt around uncomfortable questions. I don't want to have to see that little pile of bridal magazines in the basket by the television at my parents' house. I don't like the person I've become… I've always been honest. Sometimes I don't even recognise myself.'

'So, we've suddenly stopped getting along and things are tricky between us…?'

'With any luck this might be the last weekend I come to London.' She stared out of the window without blinking. 'I think when I get back home I'll just break it to them that it's over.' She turned to him and threw him a faint smile. 'I shall have to make sure I keep Mum away from the trashy weeklies. I wouldn't want her to see a picture of you in a week's time and think how fast you've recovered from your so-called engagement.'

Her voice was steady but her breathing was laboured. She'd always known that things would have to be dealt with sooner rather than later, but every word she'd spoken had still come as a surprise. It was as though someone else had decided to take charge, so that the words emerged as shocking as though they had been spoken by a third party.

She didn't dare look at Gabriel. She didn't want to see his expression of relief.

'I take it that *you'll* put in a suitable time of mourning before you move on…?'

Lucy hated that polite voice. It was the voice that told her that they were just friends. She felt she might hit him if he suggested that they keep in touch…as *friends*….

'Mum and Dad will understand. They know that not everything works out according to plan, and I've learnt a lot from this.'

'Enlighten me.'

'Well, for a start, it's made me see that one small white lie can snowball,' she told him truthfully.

Her mouth was talking and making sense, but all she could see was the void opening up in front of her. Their last weekend. The ring of finality made her feel sick.

'When I meet the man of my dreams I'm not going to play any games or tell any little white lies.'

'The man of your dreams…?'

'There's someone out there for me. A soulmate.'

'So romance is alive and kicking still?'

'I have to believe in it or else what's the point? I know you'd never understand, Gabriel. We come from different planets as far as that is concerned. Who knows? Maybe there's someone out there for you, too.'

Her heart squeezed, but she was proud of her control and of the way she was handling a horrible conversation. She wondered what this mystery woman would look like. A sexy brunette who wore the kind of clothes he liked and enjoyed all the presents he would give her. He had noticeably stopped offering to buy *her* things. Clothes, bits of jewellery, sexy underwear. All of that had become inappropriate, but she had discovered she missed the relentlessness of his offers.

'Who knows…?' Gabriel murmured. 'But in the meantime I have something of a surprise in store for you.'

'Oh? What is it?' She'd been enjoying working herself into a lather and was disgruntled at his interruption.

'Brace yourself. I've had a phone call from your mother.'

'What?' Lucy looked at him in consternation. 'Why on earth would my mother phone you?'

'Because I'm the other half of this crumbling relationship.'

'I'm not following you.' In her head she was frantically trying to slot in this new development. Just when she'd thought she would be stepping off the rollercoaster ride, allowing herself time to get used to being back on firm ground, it picked up speed.

'Your hints and insinuations did their job. Your mother thought she would phone me for clarification.'

'She *what*?' Lucy stared at him in dismay. 'This is your fault! You...if you hadn't been so charming... I didn't even know she had your number! Did you back me up?'

'Apparently I'm about to embark on a considerable amount of travelling...?'

Lucy flushed. She had meant to steer clear of that particular excuse, but she had somehow found herself in a tight spot and had blurted out the first thing that came to her head.

'I had no idea I was supposed to run with that one,' Gabriel was saying. 'For starters, where do you intend to ship me off to?'

'You *do* travel a lot with your job....'

'But relatively little compared to the amount now looming on the horizon, apparently....' In fact, his overseas travel had become remarkably curtailed. He had discovered that ruthless delegation had its benefits.

'What did you tell her?' Lucy asked in a small voice.

'I told her that it was a conversation best had on a face-to-face basis.'

'Okay. Right.' She sighed and leaned back with her eyes closed. 'It'll all be fine once I've explained that we're no longer an item.'

'Because I'm the creep who wants you to change for him, and on top of that I won't even be around to see you because my job will be taking me to all four corners of the globe for most of the year? I'm not surprised all the lying is beginning to get to you. For someone who has always been honest, I must say you show immense talent for being creative with the truth.'

'I never said anything about you being a creep,' Lucy told him defensively, still keeping her eyes closed as a sense of weariness settled over her.

'You didn't have to. It's implicit.'

'Please let's not argue over this, Gabriel. We both know that there isn't a choice. It would have been better if I had just told the truth when you came to visit and met them for the first time. If I had told them the truth then, they would have been over it by now.'

'And you would have embarked on your glittering new life? You have a point. Maybe that was a misjudgement. But what's the use crying over it now?'

'So is that the surprise? That my mother phoned?'

'They're in London.'

'What?' Lucy sat up, her heart beating very fast.

'I asked them up.'

'What on earth *for*?'

'I felt that if I was about to be shot down in flames for being a bastard then I should be around to have some input.'

'Why? What for? You won't be seeing any of us ever again!'

'Call me egotistical,' Gabriel gritted in a hard voice, 'but I don't care for the thought of my reputation being dragged through the mud with your parents.'

'Until recently you wouldn't have cared less!'

'We've already been over that old ground, Lucy. Let's move on from there. Your mother wanted to know what was going on.'

'Was she upset?'

'Bewildered. Apparently everything was fine and dandy last weekend, and then suddenly there were problems—

insurmountable problems. Your timing has been less than spectacular.'

'How can you just…*sit there* and be so calm about this? Why didn't they tell me that they were coming to London?'

'I expect they thought you'd try and talk them out of it—or maybe they just wanted to talk to me without you around, throwing them your side of the woeful story,' Gabriel said drily.

'So what do we do now?' Lucy threw him an accusing look from under her lashes. 'Where are they staying? Where are they now? Are they at your house?'

'No, they're not….'

Lucy looked at him, perplexed. 'Well, where *are* they? No, don't answer that—just tell me what you've said to them….'

'You mean so that we can get our stories straight?'

Lucy flushed. He had moaned about the person she had become, and now he had contrived, in that one sentence, to bring on a heady rush of guilt. 'You should have told me that they would be here,' she ploughed on valiantly. 'I know it's horrible to be sneaking around, pretending to be something we're not, but we both agreed that we had no choice at the time….'

'However, let's not forget that *you* were the one who generated the situation in the first place….'

'Yes, well…'

'I've told them that we definitely come from different worlds….'

Lucy breathed a sigh of heartfelt relief. 'You have so much…I could never adjust to your lifestyle—plus I'm not materialistic. I would never completely understand how someone can spend their whole lives motivated by money….'

'Just for reference—and apologies for dragging you

down from your moral high ground—if you'd been raised by someone whose finances were a source of constant change you might be a little closer to understanding….'

Disconcerted by that personal remark, Lucy stared at him.

'Thank goodness for the unchanging face of boarding school.' Gabriel, still leaning indolently against the car door, returned her stare lazily. 'Always nice to have a solid point of reference in a changing world, don't you agree?'

'Why do I think that you don't really mean that?' Lucy ventured uncertainly.

After weeks of amicable politeness, this detour into a more personal conversation dangled in front of her as tempting as a carrot being waved in front of a hungry rabbit. Helpless, she marvelled at how easy it was for him to draw her in. Was that what love was all about? An inability to keep her distance even when her head was telling her that it was imperative? She had the giddy sensation of walking into a trap.

'For an eleven-year-old boy, boarding school in a foreign country isn't always the most pleasant of experiences.'

'Why are you telling me this?' Lucy asked, in an attempt to regain control.

Gabriel inclined his head to one side. 'You want to paint me as morally suspect because I make a lot of money.'

'Not *morally suspect.* I *know* you're a pretty moral guy. I mean, you didn't *have* to bail my father out when our… our…deal fell through because I was a…a virgin….'

Gabriel drew in a sharp, long breath. Did she have any idea how sexually charged that innocent statement was? It brought back a host of memories that were as vibrant and as powerful as if he had just slept with her for the first time yesterday. He had to shift to ease the painful throb of his sudden erection, bulging and pressing against the zipper of his trousers.

'It must have been hard for you….' Lucy couldn't help the flare of sympathy she felt for a boy without a mother, stuck in a boarding school where presumably he had had to grapple with the language, while his father lurched from one failed marriage to another.

Gabriel swept past that wobbly interruption. 'So you see making money isn't necessarily the sign of a monster, but of the desire to have financial stability. If you're going to paint me as someone who is incapable of drawing lines, then I feel I need to be there to set the record straight…. But, getting back to the surprise I have in store for you… it has nothing to do with your parents being in London….'

'It hasn't?' Torn between lingering over that image of Gabriel as a young boy and the dawning realisation that *setting the record straight* was just going to muddy the already muddy waters, Lucy looked at him in surprise.

'Look around. Does this route seem familiar?'

Lucy obediently looked out of the window. Since stepping into the car she had not paid any heed to her surroundings. She was now accustomed to the drive through London to his house. It was always trafficky. The pavements were always swarming with pedestrians. Even in the peaceful oasis of his road, where his house stood in opulent splendour, she still always felt vaguely claustrophobic. As though the rush of people and cars, although not evident in the expensive road, thrummed under the pavements as a constant reminder that peace was only an illusion.

'I can't tell,' she said doubtfully. 'It's getting dark, and anyway, I've never really taken in where we were driving.'

'I get that,' Gabriel murmured softly. 'There were always more pressing things on your mind. On both our minds…'

He was still watching her in that closed, brooding manner that made her shiver with awareness and plunged her into nervous confusion. Could she be mistaken about the sexy undertones behind that mildly spoken reminder? She wouldn't have thought that he had a nostalgic bone in his body as far as women were concerned. He had certainly staged a terrific show of indifference towards her over the past few weeks—had complied with her demand to be left alone without any sign of hardship on his part at her decision… But was there some residual nostalgia there? Now that he knew that the farce was about to come to an end? She hated herself for so weakly wanting to explore that option.

'So where are we going?' She changed the subject, although her heart was jumping all over the place and prickles of tension were making her perspire.

Despite the fact that she had always laughingly turned down offers of presents from him, and although she had striven to ignore his teasing about her choice of clothes, her wardrobe had altered subtly over time. She had ditched her uniform of jeans and dungarees, and even though the weather had turned considerably colder she was now in a skirt and a soft, fleecy jumper. Images of him pushing his hand underneath her skirt, wriggling his fingers beneath the constricting tights and undies to find that part of her that was now growing damp, made her want to faint.

'Will Mum and Dad be there?' she pressed anxiously. She felt a twinge of treacherous resentment that if she broke the bad news to them as soon as she saw them then she wouldn't even be left with the memory of a last weekend with Gabriel. Why had he asked them to London? Why couldn't he just have phoned her, told her about her mother's concerns, left *her* to deal with it all?

Gabriel flicked back a pristine white cuff to consult his

watch. 'They've gone to the theatre. Matinee performance with a meal out afterwards. On the house, so to speak.'

'Thanks,' Lucy told him tightly.

Gabriel shrugged. 'Apparently, the last time they went to the theatre was over a decade ago.'

'That's not what I was thanking you for. I was being *sarcastic*, Gabriel. You're doing all this stuff…building yourself up to be the perfect…perfect…'

'Son-in-law that never was…?'

'We're supposed to be at each other's throats….'

'It's fair to say that you can be argumentative.'

Lucy flushed because there it was again—that soft, lazy drawl that brought her out in goosebumps.

'I expect the entertainment to be over by ten. It will give us time to visit a little property I've recently acquired.'

At a loss, Lucy stared at him without saying anything. 'I don't understand,' she said eventually. 'Why would I want to see a house you've bought? Why have you bought a house? Are you tired of living where you do? It *is* very big for one person,' she conceded, 'and of course, it's not a very friendly area—but then I didn't think that sort of thing mattered to you….'

'I like space, and I've never cared who my neighbours were,' Gabriel conceded, breaking eye contact. 'In fact, the less I know about the people who live around me the better. Nothing worse than nosy neighbours. Anyway, this house is just an addition to my property portfolio. It occurred to me a while ago that if this engagement continued any longer it might be more to your liking if we stayed there than at my townhouse.'

He flushed darkly. He couldn't believe he was actually saying this. In fact, he couldn't believe that he had bought a house he didn't need for the sake of a woman who had set him up in a phoney engagement, openly stated that he wasn't her type of guy and now, purchase complete and house decorated, had informed him that this was to be their last weekend.

He had been the model of good behaviour over the past few weeks. He had blithely assumed that she would be unable to resist what she thought she couldn't get. He had been willing to bide his time with her. Where he should have been enraged that a woman—any woman—had put him in such an awkward position, he had chosen to accept it because he had stopped fighting the curious reality that he wanted her at all costs.

Except she hadn't given in, and her obstinacy had made his desire to repossess her even more urgent.

'You bought a *house* because I was silly enough to condemn us to more weekends together for the sake of my parents?' Even for him, Lucy thought that sounded excessive, but then she reminded herself that whatever mansion he had bought would be an investment. Gabriel never did anything that wasn't fully anchored in firm logic and reason.

'I buy a lot of property.' Gabriel's lips thinned. He loathed the lack of control that prevented him from walking away from her. He knew he should have walked away a long time ago. In fact, he should never have made love to her in the first place. Any woman who was a virgin at twenty-four promised to be difficult in one way or another. He hated difficulties on the emotional front. He liked keeping things as uncomplicated as possible in that particular area.

'I thought you would have been more interested in places in the city centre.' Lucy was beginning to realise that they were no longer in the busy, fashionable part of London beloved by people who enjoyed showing the world how much money they had. 'Actually, I'm sure you once told me that you only invested in commercial property, and that most of it was outside the UK….'

'A change is as good as a rest,' Gabriel muttered.

The car pulled down a side street and finally drew up in front of a small detached house with a white fence, against which was pressed lots of foliage. In the dark, Lucy couldn't quite make out the individual species of plants.

'This is *it*?'

'There's no need to sound so shocked,' Gabriel said irritably. 'I'm not a completely urban animal.' His sports car was parked in the small drive.

'Yes, you are, Gabriel,' she teased cautiously. It felt good to break away from the guarded politeness of the past few weeks. 'Open spaces and too much green make you nervous.'

'You're so literal when it comes to interpreting what I say.'

He unlocked the front door and Lucy stepped into a picture-perfect house—except it was nothing like his sprawling mansion in Kensington. In fact, in some ways it reminded her of her own cottage in Somerset, although this had obviously been done up to a much higher standard. The flagstone tiles in the hall gleamed, the walls were newly painted and, glancing sideways, she could see a cheerful sitting room with an open fire. Only the presence of expensive silk rugs, similar to those in his other house, reminded her that this little gem carried a mighty price tag.

'What do you think?' Gabriel hadn't moved from the closed front door, against which he was now leaning with his hands shoved in his trouser pockets.

'I can't believe you would invest money in a house like this,' Lucy said truthfully. 'But then I suppose you have a team of people working for you who do stuff like this…

source rentable properties…make sure you're not throwing money away on something that isn't going to pay off….'

'You have such talent for seeing the worst in me,' Gabriel murmured.

Lucy pinkened but remained silent. The truth was that she loved him so much she could only see the best in him—past all those traits she once considered faults.

'Explore,' he urged, pushing himself away from the door.

Lucy almost didn't want to. Already she liked what she saw and it was painful to concede that she would be destined to have no more than one weekend in it. She noticed that he still couldn't bring himself to come close to her, and was ashamed to realise that if he reached out and touched her she would fling herself back at him without a thought for the consequences.

Very much aware of him behind her, she made her way through the downstairs of the house, which was bigger than it looked from the outside. His other house was a testimony to open space, clean lines and minimum clutter, but this was a honeycomb of exciting nooks and crannies. The kitchen, at the back, even had a bottle-green range, and she stroked it, loving the feel of the warmth under her fingers.

'There's a garden,' Gabriel said awkwardly. He sidestepped her to the conservatory leading off from the kitchen and stepped through the French doors, letting in a waft of chill air.

'Wow! It's big, isn't it?' She strolled outside, hugging herself against the cold. Fairy lights illuminated a perfectly landscaped garden, complete with a bench under a weeping willow.

'If this so-called engagement was going to continue, I figured it would be a good idea to have somewhere you could bring the mutt….'

Lucy spun round to look at him. 'Really?'

'Made sense,' Gabriel told her with a shrug. 'My house wouldn't work, and you made the point on more than one occasion that you didn't like leaving Freddy behind….'

'So are you saying that you *specifically* picked this place out with me in mind?'

In a heartbeat Gabriel realised that there was no room for prevarication, and that his usual automatic cool withdrawal from any question designed to pin him down wasn't going to work. He was a man who could handle any competition in the business world, who could face down anybody rash enough to think that they could take him on, but right now he was powerless against the earnest enquiry in those big green eyes. The woman had managed to worm her way through the dense walls of his self-imposed fortress, changing all the rules.

'Something like that, I suppose,' he conceded grudgingly. 'Of course places like these can be rented in a second….' he was compelled to point out. 'Have a look around the rest of the house. Upstairs. Your parents are in one of the guest rooms.'

'I can't believe they never mentioned a word of this to me…. What did they do last night? Did they talk to you about…about…?'

'No, they didn't,' Gabriel said shortly. 'I wasn't about to engage in a long conversation in your absence. Besides, I'd already gathered that I'd been painted into a corner. Problem was, I didn't know what the corner was supposed to look like. There seemed no point fabricating stories about trips to China if I was supposed to be setting sail for the New World.'

Lucy nodded and followed him back into the house. She was still reeling from the thought that he'd had personal input into the property—that he had bought it with her in mind. Did that indicate that perhaps he actually wanted their relationship to develop? He hadn't touched her, or even come close to touching her recently, but then again he hadn't run screaming into the distance either…. Surely for a commitment-phobe like Gabriel an engagement foisted upon him would have been the final straw, however great the sex between them was, but he had stuck around. What did that mean?

She opened doors to three bedrooms—one with angled old timber beams—and a generous-sized bathroom, before finally walking into the master bedroom, where she stopped dead at the bed of her dreams. A king-sized four-poster, the last word in romantic luxury. Eyes shining, Lucy spun round to look at Gabriel.

'You chose this especially for me?' she breathed in wonder. Hope pushed through the layers of disappointment.

'It's not a big deal. You once said you liked four-poster beds. In fact, more than once. Several hundred times.'

'So what does this mean?' she demanded as she looked at him searchingly.

'What are you talking about?'

'If you got this…for me…for us…'

'It's a four-poster bed, Lucy. Not a marriage proposal.'

Hope was extinguished as rapidly as it had taken root. What on earth had she been thinking? That a wildly extravagant show of thoughtfulness indicated a deliberate act of commitment? Had she lost her senses? Beds were about sex. He didn't want to see where they were going! He hadn't become a convert to the possibility of long-lasting relationships that led to the altar! He had stuck around, keeping a careful distance, because he still wanted her and his intention was to get her back into bed.

'A four-poster bed for me?'

'A four-poster bed for *us*.' Already he was picturing

her in it, her long blond hair splayed out around her, her small, perfect breasts pouting up at him, her slender body waiting for his attention. She was made for a four-poster bed. 'I chose it myself.'

'You haven't come near me for weeks....' Lucy was cold inside and getting colder by the second.

'You wanted me to back off,' Gabriel said softly. 'I did.'

'Did you think that I wouldn't be able to last? That I would crack?' She thought how often she had come close to doing just that and thanked her lucky stars that she hadn't. 'And, when I didn't, did you think that you could tempt me back into bed by buying this house and furnishing it with a great big four-poster bed? Just the kind of bed you knew I would like?'

Gabriel frowned. 'I've never had this much personal input into anything I've bought for a woman.'

'And you don't get any brownie points for doing it *this* time!' Lucy shouted. 'I'm not going to be your mistress until you get sick of me just because you bought a house and a four-poster bed and chose it all yourself!'

'Since when is it a crime to do something I think you'd like!' Frustrated, Gabriel raked his fingers through his hair. 'You've kept me at arm's length, and I've respected that. But keeping each other at arm's length is something neither of us wants. So you want to start hunting down your soulmate. Specifically where do you intend to pin him down? And why be a martyr in the meanwhile? Okay, so the whole phoney engagement thing adds a complicated dimension, but there's still chemistry between us. You can't deny it. Why don't you accept my gesture for what it is and enjoy it?'

'It's not what I *want*!' She could have flung something at him. One of the cushions on the bed. He wasn't a man for *cushions*! How had he dared to think that he could entice her back between the sheets by throwing a couple on a bed? 'As soon as Mum and Dad get back I'm going to tell them that it's over between us. Tomorrow morning we're going to leave first thing, and I never, *ever* want to see you again!'

CHAPTER TEN

IT WAS A MONTH before Lucy was forced to admit to herself that her mantra of never wanting to set eyes on Gabriel again was a sham.

True to her word, she had left with her parents early the following morning after her stormy argument with him. The house had been empty. Gabriel had left even before her parents had returned from their theatre expedition and he had failed to reappear.

As soon as they had returned to Somerset she had sat her parents down and haltingly told them the truth. What had started as a fling had been turned into an engagement because she hadn't wanted to stress them out or, if truth be told, face their disappointment. They had old-fashioned beliefs and she had never given them cause to question that she didn't share those beliefs. Had she been more of a rebel, she thought to herself, she might have had that fling without a conscience—but that was a passing thought that didn't have the substance to take root. The truth was that she would still have fallen in love with him, despite their inauspicious beginnings, and she would still have wanted more than he could ever give her.

Her parents had listened and accepted her explanation without passing judgement. On the surface things had returned to normality. Her routine was back in place. Things were busy at the garden centre. Christmas was just around the corner. There should have been little time to dwell on the emptiness that engulfed her, stifling her usual upbeat nature like creeping poisonous ivy.

Unfortunately, questions had begun to push themselves to the surface, and it didn't seem to matter how hard she tried to shove them back down, they still kept rising up until she could barely function.

He might not have had the vocabulary to tell her that he wanted a proper relationship with her, but hadn't he, effectively, *bought her a house*? Who did something like that if he was completely detached? And he had chosen everything inside it. Or at least some of the things inside it. Definitely the bed. The four-poster bed he had known she would adore. He had made sure that the house had a garden—somewhere for Freddy. If actions spoke louder than words, then hadn't he been trying to tell her *something*?

She hated herself for not being strong enough to make the right decision and stick to it. Or to make *any* decision and stick to it! She resented the fact that she just couldn't help trying to analyse a way out of the paralysis that had overtaken her. She couldn't sleep at night. Sometimes, during the day, she found herself drifting off into all sorts of imaginary scenarios as she tried to wrestle with the unwanted questions that kept bobbing up to the surface.

She decided that she wouldn't tell anyone when she finally made up her mind to go to London and see him. She could barely credit to herself that she was going to do it, never mind broadcast it! And she certainly wouldn't breathe a word to her parents. Things still felt a little weird with them, even though his name never passed their lips. She had the feeling that they were *concerned* for her, and their concern lay between them like a big black cloud. She had a sneaking suspicion that the smile she always made sure to wear wasn't fooling them.

She left one of her friends to look after Freddy, and it was a freezing, blustery Saturday afternoon when she boarded the familiar train to London.

She hadn't thought through what she would say to Gabriel. She didn't even know whether he would be in or not. But she didn't want to lose the element of surprise by getting in touch with him. She was firmly convinced that he wouldn't want to have anything to do with her, but she couldn't spend the rest of her life with nagging doubts as to whether she had made the right decision or not.

If she showed up and he chucked her out, then at least she could retreat as the wounded party and have some sort of closure.

Her heart was beating like a jackhammer when, hours later, she was standing in front of his house. It was a little after six-thirty and already so dark that the street lights were on.

She pressed the doorbell before she could talk herself out of it. She had passed the train ride telling herself that this was a win-win situation. Either he would hear her out, and then they could do what she knew she wanted, which was simply to enjoy each other, no questions asked, or else he would slam the door in her face, in which case, she would at least have tried.

She couldn't recall why she had been so sanctimonious. It just felt important to see him.

She was so busy trying to predict his reaction should he be in, and should that front door open, that she was temporarily caught unawares when the door was indeed opened and he was standing in front of her.

Her mouth went dry. Her fevered thoughts flew out of her head. She found that she was clutching her bag in a vice-like grip. How could she have forgotten just how beautiful he was? The few pictures she had taken of him on her phone, which she had guiltily looked at on a daily basis, didn't begin to scrape the surface of his compelling good looks.

'I…I guess you're surprised to see me….' Lucy croaked in a rush. She was riveted by the striking lines of his face, and only belatedly noticed that he was dressed to go out. Dark grey tailored trousers emphasised his long, muscular legs, and he wore a grey-and-white pinstriped shirt, one sleeve rolled to the elbow, the other in the process of being rolled down.

'I'm—I'm sorry,' she stammered, beetroot-red. 'You're going out…'

'What the hell are *you* doing here?'

He towered over her and she instinctively took a small step back. It had been a terrible mistake making this trip. She didn't know what she had been thinking. Her thoughts were all over the place when she heard a woman's voice calling from behind him—and then the owner of the voice sashayed into view.

In all the scenarios that had flashed through her head during the weeks since she had walked out of that house she had carelessly and conveniently chosen to ignore the most obvious one. That he had simply forgotten about her and moved on. She was starkly reminded of that now as a sultry brunette, clad in a skintight red dress that clung to every voluptuous curve, moved to stand next to him.

'Gabriel, darling, who on earth is this?'

Dark, heavily made-up eyes swept contemptuously over her and Lucy wanted the ground to open up and swallow her whole.

'No one,' she whispered in a desperate little voice. 'I'm no one…. I think I may have come…to the wrong house.

In fact…' She moved to turn away and felt a hand descend on her arm.

'Not so fast,' Gabriel growled, while next to him the brunette released an exasperated string of protests.

'Whoever the hell you are,' she said, resting a hand possessively on Gabriel's arm so that the three of them were connected through him in a oddly staged tableau, 'we're on our way to the opera! Gabriel, darling, can't this wait?'

Lucy raised reluctant eyes to the brunette, who was now pouting at him. She felt faint when she tried to think about what Gabriel would say should she come between him and his hot date. Did he feel that he had no choice but to invite her in because she had come such a long way to see him?

'I'll go….' she volunteered feebly. 'Actually, I was just passing through….'

'Isabella,' Gabriel said softly, without taking his eyes off Lucy's flushed face, 'time for you to leave.'

'But…'

'Apologies. My driver will deliver you back to your place. He's already outside.'

'We have tickets for the opera!'

'Feel free to use them. And don't forget your coat on your way out.'

Lucy looked longingly at the front door as it shut behind the brunette, and then her eyes slid to the floor. 'I'm so sorry,' she whispered. 'I've ruined your evening. I didn't think…' She reluctantly looked up and nervously took in his shuttered expression. 'You had a date….'

'You haven't said why you've shown up here.' He spun around, heading for the kitchen and rolling his sleeve back up as he did so.

Lucy traipsed behind him. This couldn't have been a worse outcome. When he offered her a drink she accepted with alacrity, and sat at one of the bar stools by the granite-topped kitchen counter.

'Was that your girlfriend?' she heard herself ask.

'Not relevant.' He circled her expressionlessly, forcing her into the awkward position of having to swivel round on the stool until she was looking at him where he sat on one of the chairs at the kitchen table.

'It *is* relevant,' Lucy whispered tightly.

'Because…?'

'Because…' She took a deep breath and stared down into her glass of wine. 'Because I came here to tell you that I'm sorry… I made a mistake… I've… I've missed you…' She drained her glass and braced her shoulders. 'There. I've said it. Now I'm going to leave and you can get on with the rest of your evening.'

'Isabella has been dispatched,' Gabriel drawled. 'Believe it or not, *you* have now become the rest of my evening. So you made a mistake…so you've missed me… Where is this heading? I'm curious.'

'No, you're not,' Lucy breathed on an indrawn breath, 'you're getting a kick out of this!'

She made to move past him but again he reached for her, this time pulling her back hard against him so that she half stumbled into his solid frame. She rested her free hand against his chest and could feel the rapid beating of his heart. Her mouth parted. She wanted him so badly that it physically hurt, but there was no way she would put herself forward as competition with the woman who had clearly already stepped into her shoes. She turned away, but he tilted her chin towards him so that once again their eyes were locked.

'You've moved on.' She heard the forlorn note in her voice and didn't care. Her eyes were drawn to the beating pulse in his neck. 'She's very attractive. I'm glad for you.'

'Are you? Even though you came back here to seduce me into bed with you? And there's no point denying it. I can *feel* it.'

'I'd never seduce anybody who has a girlfriend!' Her absence of any denial of his assumption was answer enough to his question, but she didn't care about that either. She was hurting everywhere inside. She could only think that once she got back on that train matters would finally be sorted.

'Isabella isn't a girlfriend,' Gabriel told her abruptly, and just as abruptly released her to pour himself another drink. Two in quick succession. Never had he needed them more.

'But you were on a date…'

'The third in three weeks.'

'Thank you for that, Gabriel.' This time she met his eyes without flinching. 'That's *just* what I needed to hear. That I was so forgettable.'

'Forgettable? No. Never that.'

'I should leave.'

'You were going to seduce me. Would you feel free to put that into action if I told you that the three women I dated, I dated once, and I wasn't tempted into bed by any of them?'

'Is that true?'

'What happened to those principles of yours? What happened to Mr Right lurking round the corner?'

'I don't care if you don't want a relationship with me.' Lucy had nothing to lose by finally being honest. After all the little deceptions along the way it was a cleansing feeling. 'I don't care if we have some fun for a day or a week or a month. There's no longer any cloud of a phoney engagement. I guess, *yes*, I came here to offer you the no-strings situation you wanted….'

'I think,' Gabriel held her eyes with his, 'it may be a little too late for that.'

'So you *did* sleep with one of those women…you *are* involved with someone else….' Ice-cold resignation pooled inside her and she couldn't get past it to convince herself that at least they were well and truly finished.

'I told you,' Gabriel said huskily, 'I didn't. If you must know, I couldn't…'

'What do you mean?'

'A kitchen isn't the place for this type of conversation.' He drained his glass and debated whether to go for the kill and have a third, but dumped the idea to make his way to the sitting area. Lucy followed, bewildered.

'So?' she asked.

'I need you to sit by me.'

'Why?'

'Because I don't feel comfortable shouting halfway across the room that my libido disappeared the day you walked out of my life.'

In a daze, Lucy teetered across to the sofa and subsided next to him. She badly wanted his arm around her but he sat forward, his hands resting loosely on his thighs, and when he spoke he addressed the ground, so that she had to lean towards him to catch what he was saying.

'I didn't expect you to come,' he threw at her, 'and I wouldn't have chased you. Hell, I figured that, with your exit, my life would get back to normal. So you wanted to hunt down your soulmate. Well, good luck to you! But nothing got back to normal, and now here you are….' He inclined his head to one side so that he was looking at her askance.

'Except the no-strings-attached relationship I'm offering is no longer on the cards,' Lucy intoned dully, and he gave her a crooked smile that had her craven pulses racing. 'I blew it.'

'Let me explain how I never wanted any kind of committed relationship with a woman. Hadn't even contemplated such a possibility. But then *you* happened, and I'm telling you now that a relationship with all the strings you can find attached is the only relationship I'm willing to accept from you.'

'Sorry?'

'You want me… Well, you'll have to get your head round the idea that I'm the guy in your life. I'm the main event. You take me on and your search for Mr Right is down the drain, because I'm going to tie you down for the rest of your life. There won't be anyone else and there's no compromise, no deal to be done.'

'I don't understand. Why would you want that?'

'Why do you think?' He gave a low, dry laugh. 'I'm in love with you, woman. I should have known as much the second I started thinking about you and houses, picturing you on that four-poster bed, getting stressed over whether you would like the garden, whether it would be big enough for the mutt…. And then keeping my hands off you…trying to prove to you that I could be the one… I didn't even know at the time just how important it was to me that you realised that, but I was going to give it a damn good go.'

'You're in love with me…?'

'I could have gone out with a hundred different women when you left and the net result would have been the same. They would have bored me to death. I've spent the past few weeks thinking about you and telling myself that there was no way I was going to show up on your doorstep and open myself up for being knocked back.'

'You love me…. You're in love with me….' She reached out and laced her fingers into his hair. Her heart melted at the searching, open look he gave her. 'I fell in love with you ages ago,' she confessed in a husky undertone, 'and it scared the living daylights out of me because I knew you weren't into commitment. When I went to that little house you'd bought I started to think that maybe you felt there was something more between us than just a fling....'

'And I told you that it was just a house...'

'And not a marriage proposal...'

'I still hadn't come round to the fact that life without you wasn't worth living. I wanted to stop you from leaving, but I didn't know how. And then you walked out and I found that I could barely function.' He straightened, pulled her into him and buried his head in her sweetly scented hair. 'You'll be pleased to hear that I'm functioning just fine right now....'

He took her hand and placed it on his zipper. She shivered to feel the telltale impressive bulge of his erection.

'Remember what I said about the house not being a marriage proposal?' he murmured as he swept her off her feet and began carrying her up to his bedroom. 'Would you do me the favour of ignoring that bloody stupid statement?'

He deposited her gently on the bed. It was where she belonged. It sickened him to think of her anywhere else, and it sickened him even more to think what might have happened if she hadn't shown up on his doorstep.

Would he have sought her out despite what he had said? Where she was concerned his pride was practically non-existent. Hell, he would have. The excuse would have been flimsy, but he wouldn't have been able to bear her absence.

He began removing his clothes, his dark, lustrous eyes pinned to her expressive face, which was now looking at him questioningly.

When he was fully naked he moved to stand by the bed. His big body shuddered as she propped herself up so that she could take his throbbing erection into her mouth and slowly pay it just the sort of exquisite attention that had him rearing back and groaning as his fingers tightened in her hair.

'I need you to marry me,' he told her with the driving urgency that was so much part and parcel of his personality.

He sank onto the bed alongside her and began undressing her with shaking hands. He would never have guessed how good it felt to lose his self-control like this.

'Yes!' Lucy was laughing as she wriggled out of her clothes. 'Yes, yes, *yes*!' She captured his beautiful face between her hands and looked at him seriously. 'You are the most amazing thing that has ever happened in my life. You entered it and changed it and I love you so much it hurts. It was horrible coming to London and doing stuff with you and not having you touch me.'

'It can't have been as hard for you as it was for me, but you wanted space and I was so damn scared that if I made a move you'd take to the hills.'

They hadn't seen each other in weeks and they made love hungrily, greedily, touching each other as though frantic to make up for lost time.

She was ready for him as he thrust powerfully into her, not bothering as he always had in the past with precautions. Lucy didn't even notice until she was lying pleasurably sated next to him. When, suddenly alarmed, she pointed out his omission, he laughed softly and stroked her hair away from her face.

'Would you believe last week I caught myself thinking that if I had got you pregnant you wouldn't have run out on me? So if you *do* get pregnant…' He smoothed his hand over her flat stomach. 'You won't hear me complaining….

In fact, I'm thinking that it might be an idea to start trying right away....'

'I see what you mean about those strings tying us down....' But she was flooded with joyful warmth, as though the sun had begun to shine inside her.

'And by the way—the engagement ring? You know that tasteless bauble has to hit the bin, don't you...?'

'The shop wouldn't have it back. It's in one of the kitchen drawers. I might just hang on to it as a souvenir of a very strange affair.'

'Twists and turns, my darling. Thank God we ended up in the right place. And, while we're on the subject, I'll just tell you that I *would* have hounded you—not that I don't prefer it this way. There's nothing a guy likes more than knowing his woman would cross deserts for him.... On a different subject, I know you don't like accepting gifts from me, but there's no way you're wearing anything but the best on your finger.'

He nudged his leg between hers and grinned as she wriggled against him until she was perfectly positioned.

'You're going to be engaged in style—although it's going to be a very short engagement. In fact, you might find me encouraging that trip to the vicar when we go and break the good news to your parents tomorrow.'

He lifted her hair to nuzzle the nape of her neck while his hand strayed to tease the stiffened bud of her nipple. He flipped her onto him and circled her narrow waist with his big hands.

'Better—much better. I want all my seed in you. Don't forget that we're trying for a baby now....'

Lucy laughed and eased him into her with a groan of pure satisfaction.

'You're moving fast!' She feathered kisses on his face, loving the feel of his rock-hard shaft inside her.

'I'm not one to let the grass grow under my feet,' Gabriel said roughly. 'I have you, and I want to get all those strings as fast as I can and tie you up with them. Figuratively, of course. Although I wouldn't be averse to exploring that concept in the literal sense….'

'Hmm…ruthless…' There was a smile in her voice and her heart was singing with joy.

'You bet. It's just one of those adorable character traits you can spend your life finding out about. Now, enough talking…we have a baby to make….'

* * * * *

Every month we put together collections and longer reads written by your favourite authors.

Here are some of next month's highlights—and don't miss our fabulous discount online!

On sale 5th April

On sale 15th March

On sale 5th April

Find out more at
www.millsandboon.co.uk/specialreleases

0413/ST/MB410

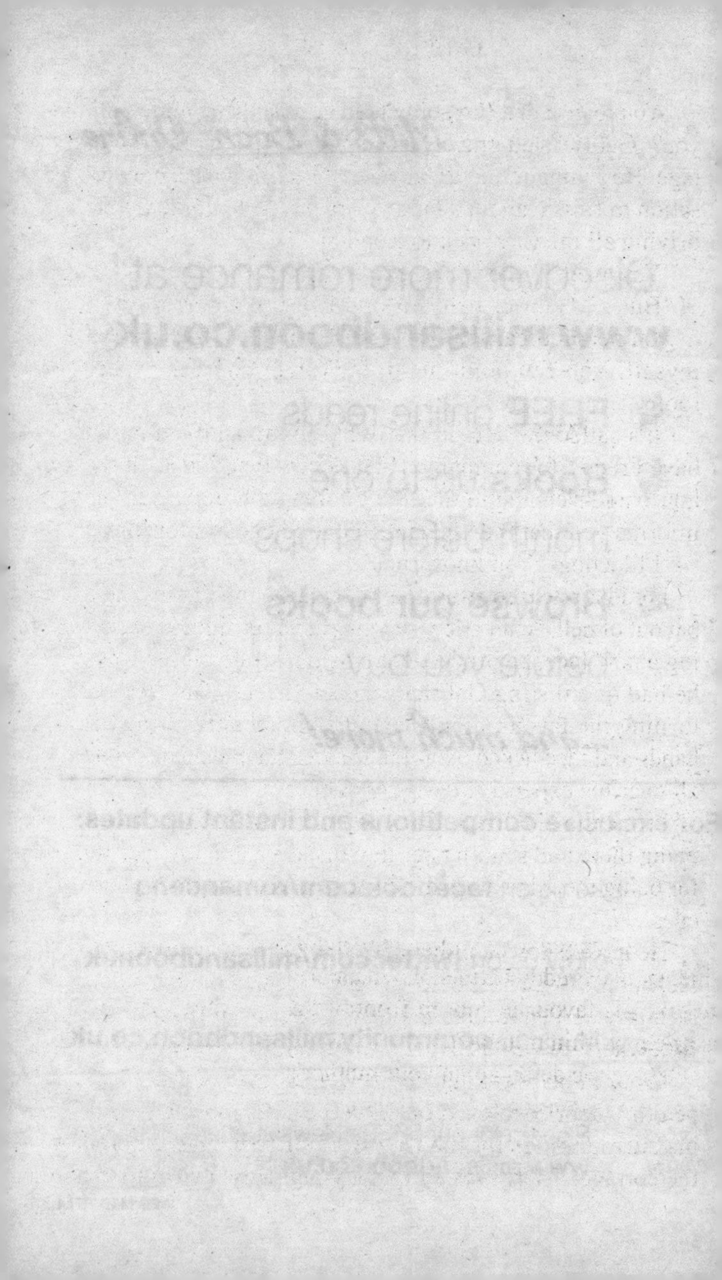